About

Sean Monaghan is the author of *Plus Ultra*. He is based in Dublin with Anne.

Also by Sean Monaghan
Plus Ultra

Planned Accidents

Sean Monaghan

POOLBEG

Published 2001
by Poolbeg Press Ltd.
123 Baldoyle Industrial Estate
Dublin 13, Ireland
Email: poolbeg@poolbeg.com
www.poolbeg.com

1 3 5 7 9 10 8 6 4 2

A catalogue record for this book is available from the British Library.

ISBN 1 84223 020 4

Cover Designed by Ridgeway Associates
Typeset by Patricia Hope in Goudy 11/14.5

Acknowledgements

Thanks to the following (in no particular order): Anne Hughes, Gaye Shortland, Dara and Mireille, T Minx, Roddy O'Hehir, Teri and Brian, Pat and Eoin, John and Carmel, Jeanie Reyes-O'Hehir, Eddy Roote, Lucy, Helen, Suzanne and Paula.

Praise for Plus Ultra

"Sean Monaghan's literary debut serves up a winding and brooding tale of sexual obsession, with a dash of death and a hint of Satanism thrown in for good measure . . . There's lots of tension in stifling heat and bustling bazaars. Choose to get an insight into the bizarre world of backpackers – and buy it now!"

Ireland on Sunday Cormac Bourke

"*Plus Ultra* is a riveting read that grips you in the first eight pages and drops you like a rag doll twelve chapters later."

The Star Terry McGeehan

"Monaghan's provocative debut is filled with elegant prose, and evokes the strange, exotic dream world of Thailand. You'll be reaching for your rucksack and *Rough Guide to Thailand* before the final chapter."

Belfast Telegraph Grania McFadden

"Sean Monaghan is a genuine world traveller and is able for the full magical mystery tour before hitting us with his punchy plot line."

Evening Herald David Diebold

"There is a huge tension and a very strong and gritty pace to it. It says something about the way the Irish novel is moving. I mean, this is not Irish writing as conventionally understood. This is international fiction."

Lyric FM Mary Coll

"We have a whole raft of funky young female writers. It's nice to see we've got a young male one to add to that."

Ireland AM – *TV3* Mark Cagney

"*Plus Ultra* is set to join *The Beach* as the definitive account of backpacking culture . . . a must-read for all budding travellers and adventurers."

The Dublin People Neil Fetherston

"*Plus Ultra* is a fine debut. His succinct, elegant prose holds the attention right through a well-told tale of a strange, dreamy Thailand. I look forward to his next work."

Patrick McCabe.

To Anne
The pre-eminent ecclesiastic of all Weltanschauung

Chapter One

BARBADOS

"It's survival of the fittest mate – and we've got the fawking gun!" Bob bellowed and fake-pounded the beer mat. His stomach was in good shape for a middle-aged father but he wore football trunks instead of swimming shorts and his big shaded spectacles nestled on his head like an upturned visor above a sunburnt bald patch. Tucked under his elbow was a large paperback: *Vampires and other stories*. His chest was laminated with tar-like hair and his flat red nose seemed to have been broken over the years in two or three places. The skin under his eyes had crumpled as if he'd walked through a thousand storms.

"Yeah." Nuala both laughed and sighed. "Where're the kiddies? Snorkelling on the beach?"

"Oh they're OK. Mel's down there to keep an eye out for mischief . . ." Bob continued talking in his hoarse soft way and he was so obviously proud of his family that Nuala didn't mind his odd glance to her deep cleavage.

The beach bar was the stuff holiday brochures are made of – thatched roof with a backdrop of warm azure waves, marble pools and palm trees. The Caribbean was so perfect that the most minor irritation took on colossal proportions. Because of this Nuala's damp red bikini bottom felt like a council flat's dry rot in the shade of the bar counter.

Nuala was twenty-eight and her hair was an on-going hobby. For this trip her thick, layered shoulder-length mane had been dyed a metallic red with a striking asymmetrical fringe. She absent-mindedly plaited a single thin side-lock and thought, Who is that guy?

He was on the other side of the bar. Three shot glasses stood to attention beside his folded arms, resting chin and cool blue one-way shades. There was a peppering of sawdust stubble over his cheeks and lip while his shoulders and smooth hairless chest were golden in an advertiser's dream kind of way. She reckoned he was about twenty-three and his sandy hair was short and tight. On top of all that, he seemed to be staring at Nuala. Well, it was either Nuala or the leggy Californian blonde piece of silicon perfection standing beside her. Instinctively Nuala inched forward her chest.

"Boo!"

Nuala shuddered and Bob shouted, "Oh Jesus!" and fell off his stool. Nuala caught the book just before it decked her umbrella-laden cocktail. Bob's ten-year-old blond twin boys hollered their way back to the beach, leaving their father perplexed and groping for his glasses, though when he found them they failed to fit his confusion. Nuala knew all eyes were on both Bob and herself: so she raised hers to the unblemished blue sky.

"Brats," he said and awkwardly laughed in his throaty way. "They'll be the death of me."

"Probably."

"Ah, you have my book."

"*Vampires and other stereotypes*." Nuala grinned and handed it back to him.

"No, no, see – *Vampires and other stories*."

"Oh yeah. Can I have one?" She took one of his Hamlet cigars and Bob flamed it while failing to hide his disapproval. Nuala asked, "How long did you say you and Mel have been here?"

"Twelve days, love. Home tomorrow night."

"Same here. Do you know who *he* is?" Nuala subtly pointed the smoking cigar to the other side of the bar.

Bob leaned in to Nuala and spoke towards her cleavage, "That's a sad young man. Wasn't talking to him myself, mind you. But Martin here behind the bar . . . he told Martin bits and pieces one night."

"Sad?" Nuala conspiratorially whispered. "Why?"

"He has extremely low self-esteem, which in my opinion is well deserved." Bob paused to gulp some golden lager. "From what Martin could pick up it seems the guy had a girlfriend and . . . well, it seems as if she was killed a few months ago and what not." He paused for another slurp of beer. "Unusual circumstances. That's all I know. Oh yeah, and he's a Paddy."

"Jesus." Nuala exhaled her smoke and wished the thick grey funnel would cross the bar and reach the stranger's face. Encrypted in it would be the knowledge that they were both Paddies who didn't like to be called Paddies. "I'm a Paddy too."

"Nooooo," he deeply gasped. "I thought you was from London. You don't sound Oirish. Hey, where's the husband?"

"Do you see a wedding band on these fingers?" She held up her left hand inclusive of cigar. "I have a great boyfriend though."

"Where is he? I'd love to meet the luckiest man on the planet."

"He's not here." Nuala sighed and sucked the foam from her cocktail. "Something awful happened."

* * *

Shane eyed the bikinis scattered around the bar. He'd narrowed it down to two. But which one to send it to? The redhead with the weird fringe, full face, nice lips and cocky gait or the Californian blonde? He knocked back his white Russian. The blonde. He reread the note just in case there were any remaining imperfections.

Hi,
I am dying.
Of Boredom.
But you are so beautiful.
Sleep with me. Please.

"Hey, Martin." Shane clicked his fingers and the black barman with shaved head, flared nostrils and a saint's civility tangoed down the bar with his stainless-steel cocktail shaker. "Martin, give this to blondie . . . yeah, the one with the tits."

"You bet, boss."

Shane looked over his shoulder to the beach. White sands, a paraglider over the blue sea, shrieks of games in the late afternoon. There were chunky splashes in the main pool as overweight Americans tossed around their similar and quite beautiful fresh brides. Shane raised his glass and threw back the rum cocktail. Beside his elbow were three shot glasses of whiskey. He didn't know whose they were, but he wished someone would take them. People were beginning to look at him as if he had a problem.

"Hey, boss – blondie send you this." The barman handed back the piece of scribbled notepaper. Shane turned it over and soaked up the freshly written word: *whatever*.

He raised his glass to the blonde Californian in acknowledgement of her raised middle digit. "Bitch," he muttered while his cheeks burned. He had no idea it would be so hard to score on this trip. After all, he was twenty-three and one of the only single guys in the entire resort. Upon touching down in Barbados, Shane had assumed it was the beginning of a ten-day shag-feast – premium drinks and food included. Instead, honeymooners and pensioners surrounded him. He'd spent most nights in the games-room, hogging the Sony Play Station, while a gang of ten-year-olds gathered around to sulkily watch him start again and again and again.

Lisa. He couldn't get her off his mind. She would've loved Barbados and this resort and that warm free feeling of all-inclusiveness. She was so perfect, enthusiastic, the engine of his existence. She hadn't lived life. She'd fisted it. And then she was kind. Lisa had been such a bleeding heart that he'd had to keep reminding her that she needed her blood to survive. Now everything was just one big dull fucking hole. Even the setting sun on the Caribbean Sea was a seeping orange sore.

Only five months ago it had been Christmas and Shane had been lucky to get a hotel in Lanzarote at short notice. Shane remembered standing at the end of the king-size bed, holding a phone, unsure of what he'd been saying into its mouthpiece. Somebody was talking at him on the other end. Reams of foreign words. He'd felt a remarkable calm despite the sensation of showering in his own goosebumps.

Lying at his feet was Lisa. Her image spread beneath him like a million sirens. Lisa had chestnut-brown hair, which fell past baby cheeks and smooth forehead. The symmetry of her stumpy pigtails was always perfect. Her lips were narrow but very brown in a Brazilian way. Cinnamon eyes, large and round, reduced her twenty-two years considerably. She was smaller than Shane was, just over five foot, small laconic ass, flat on top but exquisite legs. The most perfect legs he'd ever seen. Though his favourite part of Lisa was her back – always brown and smooth, sometimes like a river, other times like glass.

Shane had crouched to his girlfriend. He touched her neck though he had no idea what a pulse felt like or where to find it. She lay arc-shaped on the ground, one foot raised up onto the closed suitcase. The side flap of her denim mini was cast back on top of itself and her bare thigh and hipbone were smooth and unblemished. There was no sign of death. She could have been asleep.

But Shane knew. Her skin was pale and already cold yet peaceful as if her face captured the crisp fracture between this life and some other. He'd touched her thigh. A footstep echoed outside along the corridor while in the distance, seemingly outside of the universe, was the seesaw horn of the ambulance.

"Ta, mate, another lager when you're ready." A deep Cockney twang in Shane's right ear.

"And a gin for Pauline!" a high-pitched twang trumpeted from the beach.

"Em . . . how do you say it?" A stiff German voice. "Ah ya, relax and throw away the calendar."

"Bladdy hell, sorry, mate, and a gin for Pauline."

Shane looked up from his book and examined the tattooed arm of the crew-cut Brit. He didn't like the English abroad. He'd punched one in the face a few years ago in Dublin – after an international soccer match. He was proud of that.

"Excuse me, *I said*, why don't you relax and throw away the calendar?"

Shane looked over his other shoulder and thought, Christ, another midlife crisis. She looked a stylish forty-year-old. Which probably meant she was about fifty. Her tight short bleached haircut didn't exactly suit her round red cheeks. Her body was well worked but pumping iron couldn't beat time's decay and her stomach drooped and was crinkled from the expansion and contraction of several foetuses. She was at least six foot and looked down on Shane even though he was seated on a tall stool.

"Sorry." Shane tried to hide his distaste with a lazy smile. "Didn't know you were talking to me."

"Ya, I was talking to you and my name is Rita. You don't swim. Instead you read and read. All the day away. Who is it? Ah, Nabakov – typical of a writer who reads too much and invents too little. Ya?"

"Well . . . em . . ."

"Ah, writing is no big deal." She dramatically shook her head and threw her hands up to the palm-leafed roof. "It is just an ass and a seat. Writers can do the history of the world on one page or the entire lifetime of a mayfly in forty volumes . . . depends on their mood. What is this one about?"

Shane hadn't read it yet. All morning he'd been just posing with the novel, turning pages until there were no more left. "Oh, it's complicated. Tough going. You here alone?"

"No, him." She pointed across the pool and above the bobbing heads of the Americans. A fat deeply tanned bald German scowled beneath an umbrella and sipped a bloody Mary. "My husband of twenty-five years. Twenty-five years! I'm married longer then you are on this planet. I am right, no? You are not English, no?"

Shane shook his head. "Irish."

As she sat down, her buttocks that had seemed so strong and firm split to the sides like two tyres losing air. She smiled and placed a big hand, still damp from the sea, on his bare thigh.

Yes, Shane thought, *at last*.

"Where is your wife?"

"Wife? Don't have any."

"You are here with family?"

"Family? No . . . I'm self-made."

"What? Look, you not-so-English man, we are both grown-ups and we know the scenes and the situations and I don't want to . . . to play around on my husband. I want to fuck around on him. So what do you think of that, huh?" Beneath the counter her fingers slithered further up Shane's leg and he felt a long sharp nail dig a shallow burrow beneath his swimming trunks. He bit his lip against the knifelike pain.

"What about him?" Shane nodded towards her husband who was now standing beneath his table's umbrella and staring with black shades. Rita reached out and gripped Shane's chest before waving to her husband with her free hand. Her husband flung down his paperback and stormed off, much to the bewilderment of his poolside neighbours.

"Do not mind Fritz. He is weak, old and limp. The idiot blames me of course. He says that the only time a 45-year-old woman isn't thinking about sex is when she's having sex. I don't know what he means."

Beneath the protruding counter Rita's hand now covered the bulge of Shane's tight blue trunks. "Oh ya," Rita whispered and squeezed. Shane stared down at his watch so as to hide a chuffed smirk.

The day after Lisa's funeral Shane remembered twisting himself into a new spot on his apartment floor. He'd tried to be brave but bravery scared him. He felt a rage at ever having let himself come to depend on one person for so much. Death is a grievance. *The* grievance. Suddenly the answering machine had kicked into life like a long dormant computer suddenly booting itself up. It was Siobhan, Lisa's sort-of-close friend. She was talking in a sort-of-husky voice about how she sort-of-wanted to see him and perhaps go for a sort-of-drink. Siobhan had always wanted Shane, the way she'd always wanted anything her friends had. She liked his early fruition and prosperity too. She made a habit out of prowling the man in the greatest hurry.

Shane had gazed at the answering machine. "I'll shave, shower, fuck her . . . then die." There was always something else to live for.

Rita's thick polished thighs slid past his cheeks and Shane's head locked into place like a plug. Rita was loud. She thrust and withdrew to the mattress and thrust forwards again. Her shaved cunt smacked into Shane's chin and he thought, I hope that hurt. But it didn't because she did it again and again. His tongue was killing him.

"You – you like my legs. You like the strength?"

Shane looked up past the creases of tanned belly and watched the throat constrict and thought how her neck-bones looked like a turkey's wishbone. "Yeah."

"They are fat though."

"No, no," he said, fearing she'd come over all insecure and just want a cuddle instead. "Just big."

"They are fat. I don't mind . . . yaaa!"

"You don't choose . . . your glands." Her cunt was weeping into his mouth and Shane tried to like the sour salty taste.

"Oh yaaa . . . fat has nothing to do with glands . . . more, more, oh ya, just there . . . a fat person never returned from Auschwitz. Fuck ya. No! Where are you gone?"

Shane needed to rest his tongue. He quickly backed away to the minibar beside the television. He opened it and grabbed a shoulder bottle of vodka with the intention of looking cool and washing his mouth out. "I didn't think you lot liked to talk about the war?"

"Forget the war. It is so twentieth-century. You must be careful not to become an alcoholic. I don't mind though.

My father was an alcoholic and he was a lovely man. A happy drunk."

Shane swallowed and smacked his lips against the bite and the burn. He really needed a mixer. "Want a joint?" he rasped. He stood with his back to the bed and stared out through the glass patio sliding door. It was only seven o'clock and already dark outside. A couple passed on their way to one of the three restaurants. With the lights off, they didn't glance in his direction.

"You have drugs?"

"Yeah – from the lifeguard. Nice stuff."

"I don't do drugs. Fritz says that they should legalise everything just so the arseholes get what they deserve. Except for the cocaine, of course. That is good for the sex. Keep that illegal so only people like you and me can get it. I am not yet ready. I want you to do something. Bend over. Put your face against the glass and spread your cheeks."

"Spread my what?" Shane swallowed. He didn't want to appear guileless.

"I find a man's arsehole irresistible."

"When did resistance enter into it?" Shane muttered. He looked at the glass and then back to the large shadow on the bed.

"Do it," Rita demanded. "Ohhh yaaaa, I see it now. And your hanging sack. You glisten, you filthy ape."

Shane closed his eyes and reckoned that the cool glass sticking to his cheek felt like superglue. He imagined taking a deep breath and trying to tear his face away but instead ripping his head in two and slumping to the floor dead. He could hear Rita in the background, her big feet thudding to the ground, the swing of those enormous sunburnt breasts, the gaping shaved pool of her steaming cunt. Oh shit, he thought, what's she going to do?

She was behind him, kneeling on the floor, fucking herself like an old man wanking over a pair of stolen knickers.

Outside, another couple passed on their way to dinner and they didn't look towards him either. At sunrise when Shane had forced himself out of bed to ensure a poolside table, the pathway was like a swimsuit catwalk due to people's uncanny ability to rise early in strange places.

"Ya, ya, I can smell you. I can smell your manhood cunt."

Shane listened to her: squelch, squelch, and squelch. He closed his eyes and pushed his ass out further as if granting a final good deed.

"Flex your buttocks. I command you. Do it. Fuck, fuck, *fuck* you."

Out through the patio glass and across the pathway something caught Shane's eye. It was the red bikini girl with the dark red hair whom he'd almost sent his note to. Her light was on and she was sitting on the bed playing cards. She flicked her fringe. She was much broader than Lisa. Lisa had had a fringe too. She'd always had a fringe. Lisa's hair had never changed outside of the eternal dispute – pigs or no pigs? The red bikini girl was alone like him in a big double room. Alone but for Rita.

Shane pulled his head back from the glass and examined the closeness of his transparent reflection. He was a ghoul in the night. A tear glistened on his cheek. Crying reminded him of his childhood and he felt the emptiness of the bold boy's corner behind the big television.

"Push your cock back between your legs. Do it. Bend it.

Between your thighs. Make your balls look as if they are going to explode. Oh ya – explode all over me."

There was a silent hysteria. He swallowed as if vile liquid life was being funnelled down his throat. Shane squinted against his reflection. His face was transparent. But his eyes were clearly white and bright. Except the centres. The centres were portholes to the night.

"This thing of yours, this arse – it is art." Rita's hot damp breath panted against his right buttock but she did not touch him.

Shane listened to Rita grunt herself to her feet. A bone cracked. She was moving away. Back to the bed. He heard the springs creak.

"Come now. Fuck me to the finish."

Shane turned to the darkness that was Rita. But she could see him and she leaned forward from the side of the bed.

"This isn't really working – Rita." Shane struggled to pick the words. "Not my thing – really." He ran his hands over his ribs to his waist and couldn't find flesh to squeeze.

Rita began to pull on her clothes. "These days the little men become stressed – not frightened. Pull yourself together. You are better than that, no?"

Shane leaned against the glass and crouched to the floor.

Rita was calm. She easily slipped her feet into her sandals without even lowering her gaze. "Don't be afraid and do not be ashamed. Fritz says that men of steel do not bend. They break. Perhaps you are Superman? No – Superboy. I am going now."

Once the door clicked shut, Shane stood up. He faced the patio and his penis pressed against the glass. The cold shrivelled it further and the sensation felt accurate. Rita walked by. She didn't turn her head. "Lovely Rita," he hummed. "Lovely Rita."

The girl with red hair was still sitting on her bed. Her red bikini was gone and a yellow towel began at her armpits and finished at her knees. "Why is she playing cards?" Shane muttered.

He grabbed his travel binoculars from the bedside locker and quickly popped the lens covers. They were tarot cards. He'd seen them a dozen times, spread before Lisa in dingy gypsy rooms sprinkled over two continents. Fortune-tellers had been a holiday ritual.

Shane focused and could just about make out The Hermit and The Two of Cups on the creased sheets before her knees. Her hand held three more cards, which she stared at. The remainder of the gold-plated deck rested on her lap. Shane moved his attention to her face. An intelligent forehead. A round big mouth with lips that moved against each other at speed. Big eyes but whatever colour they were was not discernible. Not like Lisa's eyes. Lisa's eyes were big and brown and you'd notice them from across the street.

She suddenly blurred out of focus. Shane lowered the binoculars and observed with his own eyes. She was on her feet. She stood at the base of the bed and flung the tarot deck into the air. Then, as if realising that no one but herself would have to gather them up, she slapped her forehead and paced the room while glancing at her watch. Suddenly she faced him. She stood still, her head at first slanted towards her right shoulder before changing angle towards her left. Then she lowered the blinds.

"Bollocks," Shane muttered and suddenly remembered his exposed crinkled penis.

The day after Lisa's funeral Shane had left his city centre apartment. He'd driven around Dublin City and parked his new hire-purchase silver Ford Puma in a tower parking lot. He'd sat there in the darkness for thirty minutes. Examining the passenger make-up mirror slotted into the sunshield, he'd thought of Lisa's eyes and had tried to impose them back onto it. Then he'd thought of Neil Armstrong and the time he'd met him last year in an elevator at the Soho Grand in New York. While eagerly shaking his hand and working up the nerve to hassle him for an autograph, a depression had passed between them. Armstrong's eyes – the whites – those were the only things left that had ever walked on the moon. The rest was gone: peeled away, washed away, a promontory of dead skin and hair. Shane had breathed deeply and reminded himself that if handled properly a breakdown can be a breakthrough.

Almond Beach was deserted and dark and there was a red stain on the horizon where the sun had just been. Shane stood about ten feet into the ocean with the water bobbing against his thighs. Earlier he'd watched three American divers standing at this point – before taking one more step and disappearing into the blue depths.

Shane wore his sandals and felt a twang of guilt after having crunched his way across the precious coral rocks. The bottom half of his loose white slacks was soaked and pasted itself to his legs. But his tee shirt was loose and airy.

My problem is that I tried to be everything, he thought.

I tried to keep surprising her so that she would have a reason to think I'm great forever.

Shane looked down into the water. The red and purple brain-shaped rocks were just about visible around his feet. A couple of inches in front of him were deep fathoms of black. He knew that he was precariously balanced at the top of some gaping canyon if he could just somehow minus the water.

Shane wanted to take a step forward. Just one little step. A tiny step. It was like an illogical urge to touch the grey blur of a fan.

"Hey, you."

Shane looked over his shoulder and almost lost his footing. He squinted at the white sand that the night tried to swallow. He hoped it wasn't Rita. He didn't want to see her for a million years.

"I watched you earlier . . . at the bar." She emerged from the darkness to the water's edge. Her red hair was hidden beneath a black hat. She wore a blue sarong about her waist and a matching paisley silk waistcoat with the top two buttons popped to declare great cleavage. A pair of round shades made her seem unapproachable.

Shane fought to balance himself in the low waves. Suddenly the accent clicked. "Hey, you're Irish too!"

"Duh," she said and laughed.

"What's your name?"

"Nuala."

"Are you – here alone?" Shane felt an impetuous desperation. Don't go, don't go, don't go. Some fish slithered against his ankle and nibbled. He felt a rising panic and wanted to charge forward to the immunity of dry land.

"You look as if you're going to do something silly." She was looking in his general direction rather than at him. Maybe it was the effect of her shades.

"No. Just watching the sun set. It's – em – nice, yeah?"

"Think so?" She turned and faded into darkness.

"Wait – are you – are you –" He didn't know how to finish and there was no reply.

Chapter Two

DUBLIN – TWO WEEKS LATER

Andrew was thirty and his black hair was thick and glossy and tight against his neck. His fringe rimmed the smooth plain of a broad forehead. He had perfect homogeneous teeth. Nothing on Andrew was a misfit. His nose wasn't petite or bulbous. It wasn't sharp or corpulent. It was just a nose. He had a straight broad back: a beacon to children for a piggyback ride. His brown eyes were hard and strong like the bark of a tree. They were growing more noticeable with age.

Andrew wore a tight-fitting black Giorgio Armani single-breasted suit with matching cotton shirt and a deep-blue tie. He flexed his toned well-built body and leaned back into the comfy suspension-support chair. Andrew liked his office. It was a basic state, so simple that it was a form of genius. Plus he had a much-coveted view over Grafton Street. Some afternoons, while spinning on his blue-cushioned chair and chewing his pen, he'd take it all in: the cabinets, the in- and out-trays, computer and filofax and be reassured that his office was the crude truth of the world.

Andrew began to riffle through the pile of afternoon mail. Amongst the staple brown envelopes was one yellow envelope. He picked it up and carefully slid the silver letter opener beneath the flap. Andrew scanned the typewritten print.

Lunch again overlooking St Stephen's Green? Saw you there yesterday, looking smug and innocent. There's nothing you can do that I won't know about. It's so easy to watch you. I'm teasing myself. I observe you and think, kill him now. Just walk up to him at his table. Maybe smile first as if I'm just passing by. You'd probably smile back. And then I'd stab you. But you'd make too much noise. You'd squeal and whine like a butchered calf. I guess I'd just slit your throat. Nice and easy. Lean over you from behind. As if whispering to you. We'd both face St Stephen's Green. I'd look at the view. While you'd look back to Berlin and feel your fucking life shoot from your throat. You are a dead man. But not today.

He crumpled the yellow page into a ball, aimed at the metal bin and changed his mind. Instead he smeared it across his desk before neatly folding it back into its yellow envelope.

An hour later, Andrew held up a silver lighter. He ignited it and stared into the yellow flame. He wanted to see through it to his client – as if a filter of coloured heat would show him something that was invisible to the naked eye. But after five seconds his eye watered and the flint began to burn his thumb. So he just lit the cigarette.

"What you're telling me, Mr –"

"Andrew. To *you*, Andy." Andrew spoke like a man who made important decisions effortlessly.

"Andy. Well, you sure as hell can't shorten Bosco," Bosco said. He was bald at the centre of his crown and he brushed the front strands of brown hair over the naked flesh in an eternal fashion adopted by a billion other worried men. His eyes were green and his face stern and strong and not diminished by a white medical neck brace that appeared like a huge holy collar. The lines and wrinkles on his pasty rural face and neck were so drawn that they hung towards the floor. His eyes were pale brown and his lips narrow pencil strokes. But his ears were huge, like his hands.

"You could go for Boss, I suppose," Andrew volunteered.

The lined old man with the death of his wife still a penumbra above his head covered his mouth to laugh. "Right-y-oh, Andy. Well I've heard it all and my brain is in smithereens. So much to take in. But I must say I do feel at home here. You know, son – I mean Andy – yours is the first one where I can smoke."

Andrew assumed he meant the small teakwood panelled conference room and smiled. He hated smoke and was very aware that the cloud about his head was mostly the old man's exhaled breath made visible. He remembered a recurring adolescent nightmare where his farts were coloured red and oozed from his body to take the form of smelly speech bubbles above his head. "That's because with us, *you* always come first." Andrew chewed his lower lip. He couldn't believe he'd actually said that. He wasn't used to old people. His clients were usually middle-aged, middle-class couples who'd just inherited one of their parent's life's worth.

"I trust my instinct and you're the man for me. I know Maura would have liked you. That other fellow – Niall from down the road. Something about him. Had no faith in the human race. Said everyone out there just wanted to sell me something that would suit him or her and not me. I just looked at that fella Niall and thought, now that's a cretin trying to tell me that all cretins are liars. So tell me, Andy – tell me what to go with."

The tracker bonds were dead ducks. Even the business pages of tabloids were warning about these institutionalised con-jobs. But the commission was huge and it would look great on Andrew's portfolio at the end-of-trade monthly board meeting.

"I think you should go for . . ." Andrew paused and doodled his pen. I can't do this, he thought. He trusts me. He's somebody's father. He says hundreds as if he's talking about millions. "I think you should go for the trackers."

"Show me where to sign."

"It's a long-term thing you know. At least five years."

"Makes no difference. I'll never see a penny of it. Maura always wanted to leave the girls something more than our headstones. The eldest has two wee ones. Maura adored them . . . you know the other day I asked little Eamonn if he wanted to walk on the moon when he grew up and he looked at me as if I'd two heads and asked if I meant Mars. Fancy Mars being all the rage now. Makes you realise that one day the world is no longer yours."

There were three drawers on each side of the desk. Andrew rooted through two of them before finding the resplendent tracker bond brochure. Bosco leaned over it and his face crumpled like an elderly professor trying to complete the last line of new algebra.

"Just sign there and there . . . and your address etceteras there."

Andrew stared at the ballet of his own fingers while Bosco scribbled on the first page and moved on to the next. What about Dad? he asked himself. If he were still alive, would you do it to him? What about Mam – if she could bring herself to talk to you – would you do it to her?

Andrew reached out and snapped the brochure from under Bosco's pen. A meandering line of biro bisected the page.

"I've a better idea."

"But I thought . . ." Bosco's brow furrowed and he stared at Andrew with the look of an old man suddenly determined to outlive him.

"A *much* better idea." Andrew swallowed. "You said this is for your daughters and grandchildren. Here, go for the special investment bond. Guaranteed growth, minimum risk. Does the business."

Bosco sighed and said, "Whatever you think. Maura's philosophy is – *was* – no matter what happens nothing is complicated."

"I'll remember that." Andrew sucked on his lower lip. Bye-bye, tracker. Bye-bye, horrified faces of jealous comrades.

"Let's shake on it." Bosco spat into the palm of his right hand. He smiled and his smile was huge and for the world. "I'm a countryman. Oblige me with tradition."

Andrew flinched and instantly worked out the quickest route to the nearest handbasin. "Of course. Tradition is important. Otherwise it wouldn't be tradition."

* * *

On the corner of a quiet intersection of an affluent Dublin suburb, Shane sandwiched his silver Ford Puma between two parked cars. He checked his reflection. Hair still short but thick. Stimulated green eyes. Soft, freshly shaved skin. Cool – almost. He pinched a long eyebrow hair, counted to three and plucked. He pressed the mobile against his ear.

"No, Patrick," he said. "No, no, no. You're missing the point. The genius of Red Bull is two bulls clashing. Stand back a few feet and the bulls are suddenly angel's wings. Hence the slogan, *It gives you wings*. Fucking genius. Oh yeah – that quick lunch in Phil Kerr's house went well. Nice place. And he wants four Renaissance-fodder prints for his wife's bedroom on top of the office order. Wife's bedroom! I was fucking dying, man. Hey, what am I still doing in the 'burbs? Look, man, gotta pick up some milk before I get home. Talk to you later – see ya, Patrick."

Shane got out of his car, bleeped it locked and crossed the road. He was wearing a tight black tee shirt, dark grey jacket and black jeans. Clothes hung on Shane. They didn't sit.

A garish psychedelic purple and red painted sign hung over a small shop front declaring 'Nuala's Moonage Daydream'. As Shane opened the door, he popped a gum.

"It's my face I'm concerned about." The woman who was clearly running out of middle age was irritated. "I'm sick of hearing about my neck. Don't forget about the neck and hands they say. Look at Joan Collins. You don't want to be like her, they say . . . but oh, what I'd give to look like Joan!"

Whoever was behind the counter said, "Hmmm."

Shane ambled about the periphery. The right wall was stacked with essential oils and salts for baths, body rubs and scrubs, foot creams and a row of multicoloured ceramic essential oil burners. In the glass case beneath the counter were tall, small, fat and thin, red, blue, and green candles – each one scented with natural oils.

This isn't a newsagent's, Shane thought. A large window took up the front of the shop with some plants hanging from ornate baskets. Shelves adorned the other walls and a counter propped up the shopkeeper's elbows and cash register.

Oh my God, it's her, Shane thought. What's her name again? Nnnn . . . Nora? Nnnn . . . 'Nuala's Moonage Daydream'. Nuala! It was the first time he'd seen her in full daylight. Her eyes were blue but not immediately striking beneath a jagged dyed red fringe of thick healthy hair that poured to her shoulders. Nuala's neck was strong and long. She was broad-shouldered. Long strong legs tunnelled up to broad baby-gifting hips. He particularly noticed how the drumskin of her denim begged to disappear into her body. Despite her dimensions Nuala was very well-toned and to prove it she wore a belly-top tee shirt covering her large breasts. Her taut stomach was neatly pierced with a golden ring.

"Well, I've a zillion things for your face," Nuala said and gestured to the shelves on the left wall. "Face creams, cleanser, toner, moisturiser, face masks – all contain the perfect mix of herbs and essential oils for your particular skin type. And remember these aren't coming from rusty old Polish chemical vats. I made them." Nuala jutted her head forward and beamed.

The woman scratched her chin and said, "Well, I really only came in to have a goo. Like gosh, you're a great girl and everything. But I swear by The Bodyshop. Always busy and so many people can't be wrong."

"Well, you know what I say – beware the tyranny of the majority."

For a moment the woman's face was a cavity. Then she said, "But I suppose you're just a baby of The Bodyshop. A small-scale operation of the same sort of thing."

"A very tenuous 'sort of'. Everything here is 'to go'. Made specifically for the individual. The Bodyshop had the right idea but has no personal touch. You see I never ripped off their ideas – I just steal solutions. Look, why don't you at least try this bath powder for your stiff joints? Made of citric powder and secret natural stuff. Take it and I sentence you to dream."

"Oh no . . . well, I'll think about it. Nuala's Moonage Daydream and The Bodyshop. I suppose you could say, what's in a name?"

"What's in a name? Well, an asshole doesn't smell sweet."

Shane was more stunned then the woman. At least she was able to respond with rancorous inanities. Instead Shane found himself rooted to the spot. His lips had parted and he stared at Nuala's side profile.

"So . . . what can I do for you?"

Shane hadn't noticed the woman leave. "Em – a litre of milk." Jesus, she's so hot, he thought. Ask her out.

She remained behind the counter and looked through him just like she'd done on Almond Beach with the night setting in. "Nuala's Moonage Daydream is a cosmetics deli. Lotions and potions made to go."

"Oh yeah – em, just thought that since you sold cheese –"

"I don't sell cheese. I sell blocks of home-made soap."

"Oh yeah – I knew that." Shane realised that he was still staring at her. He turned and ran his finger over the large cork lids of several powder jars. He liked Nuala's voice. Deep and hard yet most certainly feminine. It was something that should belong to a computer-game character. His head brushed against a hanging clanging wind-chime. The clatter of the chime interrupted his nonchalant humming and it was only then that he realised he had been nonchalantly humming.

"Have we met?" she asked.

"Don't think so," Shane mumbled. You're an idiot, he told himself. A dickhead. A fool.

"Sure?"

"Well, yeah . . . now that you mention it. Barbados. Em – we were in the same resort. Almond Beach?"

"That's it." He couldn't see her face but her tone sounded la-di-da. He picked up a red candle and walked to the counter. She didn't look casual. Her face was unadorned.

"I'll take this . . . thing."

"Five-fifty."

"This shop is genius." Shane dug deep into his trousers for change and wished she'd say something. He felt that there wasn't enough oxygen in the shop for both of them.

"Genius? That's nice, thanks." This time her eyes didn't

go through him or around him. Instead they met his and he felt a twang of disappointment at their blue mediocrity. She took his money, quickly counted it and put it in the till without registering the sale.

"Yeah, well . . . you live above – like upstairs?"

"No." She examined a nail. "Nearby – Hill View Estate. Why?"

"Oh, just wondering. Shopkeepers living above their shops and all that."

"I'm not a shopkeeper," Nuala replied while still examining her nail.

"Well, see ya around," Shane said as he backed out the door. You've blown it now, he thought while crossing the road. Why didn't you just ask her out? Such a fucking simple thing to do. God, she's beautiful. The way she spoke to that old bat. She said 'asshole' the way Lisa said 'flower'. So rounded and splattered with curves. No jutting edges. Swollen with sex.

* * *

The black five-door BMW lightly revved its engine at the slowly creaking gates to the exclusive estate. Beyond the iron bars and tall walls was a small maze of cul-de-sacs lined with insipid little trees and three-, four- and five-bedroom houses, all semi-detached with big cars and leotards. For most of the residents the daily conundrum consisted of whether to go for a jog or to settle for a set of tennis. Andrew hated the security gates and their presumption that if you can't succeed with the rich then you must be their enemy. And anyway they were too slow.

He zoomed forward and cursed the first exotically tiled speed bump that tested his car's suspension. Andrew's house was halfway up the first cul-de-sac. It was a two-storey three-bedroom redbrick lump, with white plastic window frames and two small patches of lawn – front and back. It had cost him a fortune.

Andrew got out of the car and pulled his briefcase free. Two different types of cloud in the sky, he thought. Cirrus clouds and cumulonimbus clouds. Look at Richard's lawn. Thick, deep green. World-champion green. And mine: snot green. Not even newborn-baby-snot-green but runny-summer-cold-snot-green.

"Lovely day, Andy." Richard, a psychiatrist, marched up next door's driveway with his jacket thrown over a shoulder and his tie removed.

"Richard." Andrew nodded over the low wooden fence.

"Dad! Dad!" Two screaming kids advanced from the front door of Richard's house like a mad orgy of camels pushing against the needle's eye. Andrew pasted his lips to disguise his irritation. In an exclusive housing estate where nothing ever happens, activity was a drama. Richard picked one of them up, squeezed it and turned back to Andrew. "Look Andy, I don't want to fall out over blocking permission for your conservatory but –"

"No problem, Richard. I understand." I may have lost the war, Andrew thought, but I'm going to win at peace, you dull, *dull* mammal.

"Just this morning Samantha was saying that it's great how we managed to keep our argument in the planning office. Well we appreciate it over here anyway." Richard's smile and tone contained a perfectly balanced permanent serenity.

"No problem . . . em, hungry now."

"Ha, ha. Hungry now," Richard said and opened his mouth to bare perfect capped teeth and laughed, making all the correct motions, constricting throat muscles and nodding his head but without any of the noise. A silent bellow.

Andrew smiled his shrug and mated the key with the door. I hate that evil prick, he assured himself. Looking at him, listening to him, psychiatry is the witchcraft of the 21st century.

Andrew's house was like a domestic theme park. A bright white hallway with varnished wooden floor contained two archways leading to the sitting-room and the living-room. These rooms were divided by a sliding door, which was permanently open. A huge wide-screen television was hooked up to a state-of-the-art music system and the black boxes of surround sound were pinned to the four corners of the room. The furniture was black; black four-seat leather sofa and matching armchairs while in the back room was a black iron dining-table with six matching iron chairs. Large colour photographs of humpback whales were framed on the walls. The entire house was cold and leaden and didn't need a bookshelf. Almost everything besides the television, stereo and framed photographs had been chosen by an interior decorator and Andrew liked it that way. The only thing he didn't like was the flat glass case resting on the marble mantelpiece, which framed a hairy black tarantula.

On the coffee table beside the sofa was a neat pile of nature magazines – all of them had at least one whale or dolphin on the cover.

Andrew carefully hung up his black jacket on the black

metal stand behind the front door. "Excellent," he said upon noticing the sealed new issue of *Cetacean* magazine poking out of the letterbox. He read its headline and muttered, "Oh my God, they've found a *Mesoplodon hectori*."

He softly jogged up the staircase. The cream doors to the two main bedrooms were closed. The third door to the smaller spare room was slightly ajar. He placed his hand on the frame and the door creaked ponderously.

"I'm home," he said.

Nuala was seated at a black metal desk, peering into a computer screen. The office chair was black-cushioned and her metallic red hair poured over the backrest. "Shit . . . didn't hear you," Nuala said. Immediately she disconnected from the Internet with a flurry of mouse clicks.

Andrew had noticed that Nuala had recently become very private about her Internet addiction. He didn't mind though. Outside of the *Whale Watch Antarctica* site, the Web bored him.

Don't tell her about the letter, he told himself. "I got another letter."

"Oh no," she said and turned around on the spin chair.

"Yeah – in the afternoon mail. Dublin postmark. Shredded it as usual."

Nuala remained seated. "I wish you'd let me see them."

"They just say the same thing – *you're dead* or whatever. But it's getting to me."

"Me too. I wish there was someone we could tell. I've been thinking – it's Matt. I'm telling you."

"Last week you said it was Sheila," Andrew said. "And the only thing they have in common is that they've absolutely no reason to send me death threats."

"No one has a reason to send you death threats. They're fucking with your mind – the little prick or pricks or bitch or bitches." Nuala's hand groped about the desk for her cigarettes. In the ashtray beside her elbow a tube of ash remained from a cigarette that had been cremated rather than smoked.

"Well, there's nothing we can do about it so let's just – forget about it. Hey, you're back online. How did you manage that? Thought the virus killed it."

"Tec support cured me. Very stressful. Listening to impatient fucks who just spend the best part of their lives trying to understand a poxy underdeveloped invention."

"Well, you're online. No more sulking."

"I don't sulk." She found her cigarettes and lit one. Andrew watched her dark transparent reflection in the computer screen. He felt like he was talking to a machine. He moved his hand in a circle before his face but the monitor still only picked up *her* image. He watched the dark reflection of her ghost transcend the bright screen as she held a cigarette before her lips as if she were about to renounce the habit as something ghastly from the third world. "I take action," she then said. "A software patch is in the snail-mail for a more permanent solution. Bet I won't know how to use that. There are many ways not to understand and Bill fucking Gates just keeps coming up with more and more. Hey, Andrew, I'm starving."

"Me too. Plans for tonight?"

"Got a vid on the way home," Nuala muttered around her cigarette, "and a bottle of wine."

"Another video? Jesus."

"I remember when you used to go out on Fridays. And

Saturdays. Sundays too and Thursdays. Now look at you – a night in with a video gets in the way of your fascinating Flipper books. Now quit bitch'n' and get into the kitchen."

"Quit bitch'n' – hey, Matt said that at lunch."

"Not before Joey said it in Thursday's *Friends* rerun."

Chapter Three

Nuala leaned back into the sofa. Am I fat? she thought. Her hands rested on her pierced belly. It was big in her eyes. But what about Andrew? Would he agree if honesty was forced upon him?

I couldn't be arsed asking him, she thought. Arsed. If the computer underlines it, then it isn't part of my life. Crap English film – this is shit. Arsed. Would the processor acknowledge that? If I eat those tinned crisps I'll feel ill. This is it. Stomach full. Nothing to do with being fat. The greatest athlete is ineffectual and bulging if she eats too much.

Nuala reached forward and took the wine glass by the stem. A nice white glow to block the deep luminescence of the lampshade. "Are you sure you don't want any?" she asked without looking at him. Her voice clung to a film of phlegm. She felt it vibrate in her throat but wondered if Andrew could actually hear it.

"No, I'm fine."

"Sure? There's Bacardi. Loads of Coke in the fridge too. Might get rid of that crick in your back."

"*Neck*. It's in my neck."

Boo-fucking-hoo, she thought. How much time? Twenty minutes left on the vid. Twenty fucking minutes. Then what? Nothing remotely interesting, that's for sure.

Nuala disguised a yawn. It felt like a fat yawn. She imagined herself alone in the living-room. The deep lampshade glow. Video playing. Andrew wasn't there. None of his sober tension. Crick in his neck. *I'm so tired*, crap.

Nuala felt a prod of the gods to reach across the dizzy chasm and pour more of that fruity wine. She thought about it. A nice long thought. But no. Definitely no.

"Nuala, know what *really* annoys me?" Andrew clutched the remote control. His hand was in her peripheral vision. Andrew pressed 'pause'. There was silence in the room. Nuala grunted. She wanted the remote control. In a perfect world she would break his hand to get it. The TV flicked the paused image and she could feel it on her tongue.

"The fact that the only good parts are in the trailer. I'm glad we're the only people in the country who didn't see it in the cinema."

Nuala grunted. Andrew's fingers liberated the remote control to the comfy cushions between them. His finger tapped 'play' and the room once again flickered with energy and sound.

"Take some wine." She gestured to the distant bottle.

"No. Shhhhh."

* * *

Shane loved his two-bed city centre apartment. It was ten storeys up at the top of his block and overlooked the River Liffey. Standing to the right of the front door was an ornate bronze statue of two entwined lovers supporting an orange cut-glass lampshade.

In the living-room, mahogany shelves supported a library. The library was divided into topics such as history, geography, medicine. Even then the hardback spines were arranged alphabetically by author. When Shane had first moved in he'd owned one book – the paperback *Harlot's Ghost* by Norman Mailer, which was as big as a hardback. Lisa had noticed that it fitted perfectly onto the barren shelves. The next day she'd walked into a second-hand bookshop with *Harlot's Ghost* tucked beneath her arm. There, she used it as a chunky measuring tape when picking out twenty books to decorate the walls with. A month later, after countless visits to bookshops and suburban parish fairs Lisa had collected a very impressive library.

There was a large ornate mirror above the raised mantelpiece. Silver swirls of fatuous design reached for the roof while the only useful part – the glass – was cut into the shape of a diamond and therefore limited the extent of the whole-self in the reflection.

Almost naked, Shane sank into the sofa of the darkened room. He slipped his hand beneath the front elastic of his white C K boxers. "Entertain me," Shane said to the television and picked up the game-console from the ground. He released 'pause' and the screen zapped into life and sound. A half-empty bottle of Bud rested between his thighs. Covering his groin was the joystick which he clutched like it was a doll or a penis. A physical depression still remained beside him from Lisa's absent buttocks.

His thoughts returned to the night Lisa had been killed. He remembered everything about Lanzarote. They had hurried along Avenida de las Playas and past the bars and restaurants overlooking the drear of night that was Blanca beach. It was Christmas and while bracing themselves for a lack of saturnalian revelry, they were surprised at the number of tattooed English families, conspicuous with Santa hats and flashing reindeer horns, rooted to ridiculous Union Jack bars.

So it was in a neutral lounge that they'd first met Soeren Halkier. He was a twenty-year-old Norwegian who made Shane feel like an old fart at twenty-three. He was beautiful rather than handsome. His hair was thick and messy in a very technic way. And he was tall and slim and liked to elasticize his body. Soeren Halkier's eyes were brilliantly blue. Shane didn't like Soeren because Soeren claimed in stringent English to adore the contemporary art scene yet had never heard of Rothko and thought Julian Schnabel was only a moviemaker. Soeren Halkier liked Dali.

Soeren was already at the Centro Atlántico bar – occupying a glass-topped table on a balcony overlooking the teeming pavement. He waved and Shane's stomach tightened. He didn't know why. Soeren seemed more eager to impress than to overawe. But still his stomach hurt and he subtly rubbed it through the thin fibre of his white silver-buttoned shirt.

"There he is," Lisa said and tittered under her breath. Her big eyes were wide which made them huge. Shane couldn't help but sometimes see her as a sister and he – a long-lost but perverted brother.

"Yeah great," Shane muttered behind a smile and a wave. He gently patted her ass. At least Lisa was in better form. She'd been ill with some bug for most of the week.

Headaches, high fever, diarrhoea. The previous day a sunburn-like rash on her back was almost the last straw. It had taken Shane all day to talk her into staying for the rest of their Lanzarote Christmas holiday.

Soeren had already bought the drinks. A thin-stemmed and broad sugar-rimmed glass contained Lisa's piño colada complete with chunk of raw pineapple and fire sparkler, which he immediately ignited. A bottle of Bud for Shane.

"Hello, Shawn."

"Shane. It's Shane."

"Oh, *Shane* – not Shawn. Not so good with the names at the beginning." He turned his head to the blushing Lisa who had taken a seat on his left side and said, "But I remembered yours, of course. A simple thing to remember."

Shane sat opposite and lit a cigarette, wishing it were a joint. His stomach made a noise but no one heard. Shut up, stomach, he thought. Lisa was already sucking on her straw and Soeren clinked Shane's stationary bottle of Bud with his choice of whiskey. Shane's eyes narrowed. When Soeren smiled, he smiled like a teen-idol.

"So, Shane, last night I told you why I am here. At least I have an excuse, huh? What about you and your girlfriend? Why are you here?"

The sensation of a minor internal land-spill made Shane twitch forward and for a second he caught Lisa's eye. She was leaning around Soeren's shoulder trying hard to be involved. She was biting her lower lip. "With the art business it's hard to know when you can get away until the last minute," Shane said. "But when the last minute came this was the only little rock on the whole fucking planet with a temperature even slightly higher than ours . . . with a vacant room. Nice hotel though. Lisa, tell him about it."

Too eagerly Soeren turned to Lisa. Shane lifted his beer bottle and took a sip. "Another round?"

Neither acknowledged him. Pricks, he thought. Well, not Lisa. Not with that thong hidden beneath her black mini, beneath this glass table top, a few feet from my reach. Has Soeren thought about what lies in that darkness? Bet he has – the cunt.

Shane grabbed his cigarettes.

The bar was too packed. The waiters were rude and getting in his way. He passed the long claustrophobic drinks counter and descended the narrow stairs. There was a poolroom and a gang of quiet young brown locals clicked their sticks against the coloured balls. The toilet. Three urinals were entertained and Shane's elbow hurried against each man's shoulder as he squeezed by and he muttered, "Scusi, scusi, scusi".

Thankfully the sole cubicle was vacant and he slammed its door with one hand while the other grappled with his trouser button.

"Fucking shellfish," he muttered. Then Shane heard an echo. It ricocheted three times before quickly fading. The door was only a few inches from his face and he wiped a layer of sweat from his brow. The air was stale, warm and quiescent and the cubicle felt like a high attic in summer. The echo vibrated again and Shane tensed because it sounded forlorn. It was just one word muttered twice by the same man – "Ahhhh".

Covering his eyes Shane breathed into his palms as if they had become a paper bag. Nothing happened despite feeling a moment away from a violent evacuation but the second just stretched and snapped and Shane pulled up his trousers. He hated the fact that keeping control of himself was not always automatic.

Shane snuggled wounded-like onto a stool at the corner of the bar. He worked a visual tunnel through various upper body parts back to where he could just about make out Lisa and Soeren at the glass-topped table. They weren't missing him. There was laughter and he saw a kittenish Lisa lean into Soeren and elbow him. The Norwegian responded by tugging on one of her stumpy pigtails before continuing to flirt like a devil who had just discovered his one true angel.

Shane lit a cigarette, inhaled and did not enjoy its taste. Suddenly Lisa was scouting for him. She stood up and the raised floor made her tower over the bar. Shane waved and watched as she began to wince her way through the crowd. Finally she reached him and asked, "What's keeping you?"

"I'm –"

"Soeren Halkier," she giggled, "what a stupid name! Why couldn't he be called John or something? C'mon back and talk to him. He likes art, remember?"

Shane grunted. "I've gotta go." He palmed his stomach for effect and for a bit of sympathy. "Not well."

"Oh Jesus." She looked to her feet and tried to sound concerned with, "Are you all right? Is it serious?"

Yes, it is fucking serious, he thought. "Nah, just a baby version of whatever you had. A twenty-four-hour thing. But I can hardly keep my eyes open."

"Right, let's go." She audibly held her breath.

Shane smiled and took her hand. "You stay. It's no big deal me going." Shane dropped a hand and lightly rubbed his forefinger up a recently bronzed thigh.

"Poor Shane, are you sure you'll be all right?" She patted his cheek. "And you *want* me to stay? This is definitely what *you* want?"

Of course it isn't, he thought. "Lisa, you *know* it's what I want. I'll be waiting." His hand rested on her hipbone and it was always a surprise that it wouldn't squeeze when he tried to squeeze it.

Soeren Halkier took it well. In fact, news of Shane's illness seemed to spur his own energy level a notch or two and he made himself perpendicular on his seat and nodded sympathetically. "A good sleep, *Shawn*," he said flicking a long strand of fringe from his right eye. "That is all I think should do it."

Shane nodded, considered ways to mispronounce his name, came up with none and drained the spare bottle of club.

"You know what, *Shawn*?" Soeren said and grinned with subdued glee as Lisa slithered in beside him. "From what your woman tells me, you pack things in so tight that your belly can do nothing but make strange noises."

"It's Shane, by the way," Shane said while checking for his key. "*Shane*. Shane as in 'Lane' or 'Frame' or 'Shame'. Got it this time? Make sure you walk her home."

"Of course," Soeren bowed.

* * *

Shane glanced at his score in the corner of the TV screen and stretched triumphantly to his feet. He couldn't see Nuala with her hair in pigs. She was broad, big and healthy. Probably never had diarrhoea or a rash in her life. And she was cold – unsmiling. Lisa had always smiled. Even when she was miserable. "Hill View Estate," Shane muttered. "Wonder what that place is like." He wasn't tired. The suburb was a ten-minute drive away. He took a final slug from the beer bottle and wiped the Cimmerian taste from his lips. After pulling on his clothes he snatched up his car keys with the optimism of an adventurer assured of a charmed existence.

* * *

"Night-night," Nuala said mid-yawn and hauled herself from the sofa. Andrew wished she'd lift her feet instead of half-skidding across the carpet in her stupid red furry slippers. It was so lazy.

When the door clicked shut, Andrew zapped off the TV and zapped on the stereo. A CD of whining whale-sounds filled the dim yellow lamplight. He turned his attention to the hardback book lying open on the sofa beside him. The *stenella frontalis* was infinitely more attractive in its own special way than the creepy starlets in that awful film, who seemed to consider malnutrition as the most effective way to wear their clothes. But there was something vaguely unsatisfying about the *stenella frontalis*. Maybe it was the fact that Andrew knew everything there was to know about spotted dolphins. There was no mystery left. On the following page was a chapter on the *Ganges River dolphin*. Andrew knew zilch about that endangered grey beauty. Still, reading about the *stenella frontalis* didn't require much concentration. Andrew rubbed his eyes and hoped he wasn't reaching a stage in his life where he was only interested in learning the stuff he already knew.

Andrew stood up and looked at the framed prints on the walls. Dolphins in crisp blue seas. Whales shooting their spray to the moon. Nuala hated them. She'd wanted paintings. Paintings instead of more ugly whales. But Andrew had no interest in art. He had a private suspicion that most art is just men showing off. While whales were life itself. Like children. The face of a dolphin – its built-in smile and crinkled forehead. Its naked crown. Like a newborn baby. Whales were eternally newborn.

Andrew looked out the front window. He envied Richard's family. It would be nice one day to have a son or sons. But that was never going to happen. Not a chance. Andrew remembered a summer's evening nine years ago in former East Berlin. Cranes, walkways and steel support ropes criss-crossed the horizon with metal. The sky was a bluer black and stars broke through the electric light of the city. With a thousand absent crane operators the eastern district of Kreuzberg 36 was quiet.

A twenty-one-year-old Andrew stood on the footpath of Oranenstrasse, leaning against a parking meter outside what appeared to be a butcher's shop. The lights were off and the counter was bare. Above the door and painted across the windows were Arabic squiggles. His twenty-two-year-old friend, Liam, slouched beside him. Liam was gorgeous in a delicate rock-star sense. His thick healthy hair was bleached a dazzling white while his huge blue eyes were a perfect complement to a pale white face, red wet lips, crucifix earrings and a light blue second-hand Gianni Versace jacket which just about covered a smooth chest and ribs.

"This is so cool," Andrew said and clapped his hands. He wore white Levis and a black nylon tee shirt. He'd dyed his thick hair a deep red. Andrew brushed back his floppy fringe and scanned the street. No traffic except for speeding taxis blurring the Skalitzerstrasse junction. The only people around were two bar-hoppers rapidly approaching, heads down, hoods up. When they got closer it was apparent that they were in fact Turkish women, wrapped in shawls and veils, gloves and tights.

Andrew checked his watch. Ten minutes of waiting. It was the longest ten minutes in the world. The Berlin edge made him nervous. "Jesus, Liam, can you believe this is happening to us? To us! Wow – it's so – so cool."

"Fucking right it's cool. This, Andy, is what life is about. Fuck, yeah. Look at us! Everyone we went to school with is stuck in college or offices or whatever. And look at us! We're in Berlin! Fucking Berlin and we're going to be –"

A car was speeding down the street. A black Mercedes. It picked up speed and Andrew cracked his knuckles. This is it, he thought. This is it. The greatest night of my life. The car braked and the tyres screeched to a halt right beside the meter pole. The back door clicked open. A face emerged from the luxurious shadow. He was dark, beautiful, and smooth. He looked like a sixteen-year-old Asian prince, with both ears pierced and a trace of blue mascara on narrow slanted eyes. He wore a yellow velvet waistcoat. Beneath it was a hairless, brown, *very* perfect chest. His arms were fragile and flawless. A light glitter of stardust coated his entire face. His dark red lips glistened from the street lamp.

"Par-tay, boys?" A deep-south American drawl sounded from the front of the car.

Andrew leaned into the Mercedes. Two men sat up front. The driver was black and his head shaved. Beside him a white guy ogled through a large video camera.

"Come on, guys," the American with the video camera

said. "Accept a lift from a stranger. I like it when common sense isn't so common any more. Two young men like you, in this area, at this time of night – would I be correct in assuming you're both queer as hell and not going to take it any more?" Behind the camera he nodded with the experience of a thirty-second expert in everything.

Andrew slipped in beside the young Asian and Liam jumped in after him. The car started moving. The man with the camera was broad and jammed into a brown suit. "OK – cut." He lowered the camera to his shoulder. "This thing is meant to be wrapped and in Italy by Sunday. Jeez, guys, act more surprised. You're meant to be clubbers on the street. Christ man, ya pay peanuts and ya get fucking monkeys. Sheeesh! We'll take it from the top again. We'll do it on Hauptstrasse. Schöneberg is full of nice little alleyways for the bonnet scene. I'll paste the lot together at home. And remember, you're *real* guys. *Real* fucking guys – and – action." He picked up the camera and plugged it back into his eye. "This is the deal," he said, now speaking in a light Californian accent loud enough for the attached microphone to clearly pick up. "I'm Blofeldt-sixty-nine but you guys can call me Blofeldt. I'm making a movie here and you can do whatever you want with this gorgeous cock-boy . . . as long as I can film it. Cool?"

"Oh man." Andrew smiled into the lens. "Oh man, oh man."

Liam leaned forward and pulled a pose for the camera. "That's cool by us. Fuck, yeah."

"More excellence! So tell the gang at home a little about yourselves . . . yeah that's it. To the camera."

"Oh, we're just nightclubbing," Liam said, pushing

Andrew back into the seat with a subtle prod of his elbow. "We're meeting the guys at Zoulou Bar and then hitting Tresor later."

"OK guys, whatever, Sam's looking bored."

Andrew turned to Sammy. His fastened waistcoat was difficult. Can't go over it, can't go through it, have to go under it. He jammed his fingers up to Sammy's chest. He pressed hard. All ribs and no tits. But there *was* a nipple and if he pinched he could gather the skin together and that felt like a mound. Andrew liked a worked-out prominent hard chest.

Liam joined in. He reached around Andrew and pulled down Sammy's gold velvet waistcoat and exposed his perfect hairless chest. Then he closed his eyes and sucked a deep brown nipple.

"Yeah, perfect man, perfect," Blofeldt muttered.

The black Mercedes cruised up Hauptstrasse towards Bahnhof Zoo. The buildings were spreads of bunker-like walls with tiny windows. Nightclubbers moved in small groups.

In the back seat of the black Mercedes a naked Sammy spread himself on Andrew. Liam's head was buried deep between Sammy's thighs. The black driver glanced in the rear-view mirror – fascinated and repulsed as if watching dogs queue to hump a lost bewildered bitch.

"Yeah, that's it, guys," Blofeldt panted from behind his camera. "Fuck the bunny. Fuck the horny bunny. That's what the folks back home are communicating to me via their psychic pumping cocks."

It was like an operation – each of them taking turns in an intense effort to save this young Asian prince's life. Andrew let his head loll back and he stared upwards and out the back window, watching the overhanging street lights whiz by like lightning. He thought of bombs, tanks and Hitler.

Suddenly a siren pierced the car's interior with blue sound.

"What the fuck!" Blofeldt shouted and lowered the camera onto the neck-rest of his seat. His cheeks were red and his white tee shirt bulged with steroid muscles. "Jesus fucking Christ, man. We're fucked!"

"It's cool," the black driver stated into Blofeldt's pinpricked eyes. "Just an ambulance."

Blofeldt wiped his blond receding forty-something hairline and whispered, "Thank Christ."

Andrew swallowed. "Sorry, Blofeldt . . . what's the problem with the ambulance?"

"Thought it was the cops. Wasn't it obvious?" Blofeldt picked up his still-running camera from the headrest.

Sammy puffed on a cigarette and watched everyone else as if they were discussing a book he'd never read.

Liam subtly pressed his leg against Andrew's and cleared his throat. "But you said the Germans were OK with this porno stuff?"

"They are," Blofeldt said. "But he's a kid. A very cute kid without a word of English and unfortunately on the verge of a dental breakdown."

The black driver laughed.

Andrew focused on Sammy's teeth. They were smeared with black decay, crooked and sharp.

"Don't worry, kiddo," Blofeldt said. "We're not talking about you. Honest. And if you're a good boy we'll give you more of those little blue pills you like so much."

Sammy squeezed Andrew's arm and blew smoke across him and across Liam before the funnel dispersed out the window.

Blofeldt leaned over the neck-rest of his seat and whispered to Andrew, "Seriously though, Sammy's greatest gift is his ambidextrous limbs – you'll see."

"If it had been the police," Liam said, "it wouldn't have mattered, right? 'Cause he's sixteen and that's OK in Berlin."

"Jesus, not again," Blofeldt muttered before speaking up. "Look, he's a kid. He's eleven. He just looks sixteen . . . the magic of shitty-lighting and heavy make-up. Big fucking deal, yeah? Kids are like Pringles. Once you pop them, you can't stop."

Andrew looked at Blofeldt and the camera. Then he started laughing. "Great . . . a kid . . . I'm good with kids."

There was a loud crash as the camera lens suddenly jumped from Blofeldt's hands and smashed against the roof. The bulb shattered and shards of glass sprayed themselves about the car. "Motherfucker!" Blofeldt shouted as the remainder of the camera fell back onto his lap. Andrew's foot shot forward again and hit the undercarriage of the camera. A dent appeared in the metal casing.

"Do you know how much that fucking thing cost me? Pull in. Pull fucking in!"

The black Mercedes indicated and pulled off the road into a small parking-inlet for the Tiergarten public park. Andrew craned his neck and looked out the back window. There were trees up above. Deciduous trees. Thick, green bunches of leaves. He could hear them rustle.

* * *

In the Dublin suburbs, Andrew squinted out the window of his living-room and down the road. A fox strutted by a parked silver Ford Puma like a creature that knew it could go anywhere under cover of darkness. Andrew withdrew the latest letter from his back pocket and quickly reread it. I don't want to die, he thought. I just want to go to sleep. Andrew clicked off the lamp and sighed like a pessimist who was just reassured that things had turned out badly.

Chapter Four

Shane stretched himself on the driver's seat and pressed his hands against the padded roof. He'd been stranded in the estate for over an hour now. And in all that time only two cars had passed through the gates – both being too slow to allow Shane time to squeeze through the temporarily unencumbered exit. The next car that comes through will let me out, he thought. I'll get out of here if it kills me. He imagined starting the engine and jamming down his foot and perhaps he would be able to register which random wall was a second away from crushing his skull.

Shane slammed his fists against the steering wheel and looked about the car. No one was around or awake. His green eyes observed the mirror. He was bored with his crewcut. Tight and sharp. His lips were wine-coloured and naturally pouted so that when he did pout they swelled like hot veins. He closed his eyes and waited for the next car.

Shane felt the gravity of his body and sensed the light shove against his eyelids. He liked the image in his head and the thoughts chaperoning it. There was noise outside. Footsteps. He opened his eyes and snapped them shut. She was coming. *Et in Arcadia ego*. Poussin's masterpiece. Three shepherds and a shepherdess staring at a tomb in the idyllic dreamland of the pastorals – Arcady. Shane opened his eyes again and the day hurt his brain. Poussin's masterpiece cinched in Grail lore. Nuala walked by the front of the car. He couldn't even register what she was wearing. Nicolas Poussin and the Grail.

"Jesus fucking Christ," Shane muttered with a sudden shock of clarity. "I'm still here."

Knuckles rapped against the side window.

He thought about starting the car and speeding off but that would just make things worse.

Her hand tapped the glass again.

Shane quickly checked the rear-view mirror and rubbed his stubble. Crusty green and yellow boulders of sleep rested in the corners of his eyes. He rubbed them. Shane pressed a button and the metal door ate the glass window.

"Think I'm thick?" she said. "Think I wouldn't be able to remember what little-boy-racer car you drove?"

"What?" Shane's tongue stuck to the roof of his mouth. He worked it free. Shane looked into her face. No make-up and her lips were still adipose and savoury and crimson. There were perfect dimples that sucked up all that baby fat. She was wearing a dressinggown. It was dark red and padded for warmth. There was nothing special about it. Shane couldn't tell what was underneath as it was fastened tight to the collar. His cock was already stiffening and the idea of an erection in this situation appalled even himself. It occurred to Shane that his veins didn't pump with testosterone: they pumped with preposterone.

"You're following me," she said. A cigarette dangled by her side and Shane immediately felt a craving. Nuala coughed into her hand and added, "Why?"

"No, I'm not. Honestly – you've got me in an awkward position."

"You're in *no* position. And remember you can't stalk anything without legs. And with your balls relocated somewhere in your gall bladder in the right upper region of your abdomen you wouldn't have the urge to anyway. Want me to phone the police?"

"Fuck no! Please – just give me a minute." Shane scanned his furry dashboard for a cigarette but there was just ash. "I swear – I swear I got locked in. Then I fell asleep. Shit. I know it sounds mad but *I swear*."

Nuala checked her watch and Shane automatically checked the dashboard clock. Six-thirty in the morning. Nuala dropped her butt and seemed to contemplate standing on it before changing her mind. "What do you want? What's on your mind?"

Shane looked into her eyes and saw a reflection of his decision to be in love. He wanted to say, what's on my mind? The same thing that's on my mind when I open my eyes to each new morning when I'm greeted by a hard-on that seems only to exist to remind me why I'm here. I see your palm touch my car door and think of it as nothing but the vessel of my testicle-receptacle.

But instead Shane said, "Look, I just want to go. I've been locked in all night."

Nuala rubbed the back of her hand across her nose.

Shane caught a glimpse of argentine moisture and loved that hint of hardcore reality. She seemed normal, which was, considering the circumstances, abnormal.

"Can I go?" Shane asked.

"Depends what you want." Nuala cracked her knuckles and despite the machismo of the gesture it did nothing but remind Shane of her femininity. Cracked knuckles and her jagged red fringe.

Shane swallowed. This is it, he thought. Tell her the truth. The truth is no big deal – you just want to ask her out. Simple. And if she says no – which she will – then at least she won't have called the cops. "I have – I have – since Barbados. And you only live once so I've tried to see what happens – I've tried to see if you and I can – I dunno, *happen* I suppose. Fuck, I'm an idiot. I really am. I *know* I am." Shane rubbed his cheek. He felt hot. His stomach was lead and he glanced down the road of sleeping wealth.

"I think it's because of your girlfriend," Nuala said and stepped back from the car so she could straighten her back. "I think that in the middle of the night you're a very lonely young man."

"No, I'm not," Shane said and swallowed back his panic and the hint of immediate rage. Lisa. How does she know about Lisa? "I've loads of mates."

"Really."

"Em . . . are you asking me a question? Can I have a cigarette?"

"No and no. You'd better go. People don't like weirdoes in this estate. Even if they look like you and drive flash cars. The ex-Tánaiste lives over there." Nuala pointed to a corner house. "See? Remember the guy with stupid teeth?"

"Nope – never voted in my life."

Nuala laughed.

Shane said, "Can we meet? Like, sometime at a reasonable hour?" There, he thought, I did it.

Nuala scratched her head and said, "I'll have to think about it first." She pointed a small black box towards the impressive security gates in the distance. Immediately they started to creak. Then she turned and walked away. Shane watched her round pond-like buttocks piston her body across the road. Not even a chunky dressing-gown could contain her sex. Shane started up the car. He turned the radio on, not to hear music or chat, but to hear anything.

* * *

Nuala's Moonage Daydream was empty which was not unusual for a Saturday afternoon. Nuala stood before the front window and scanned the quiet suburban intersection. The area around Nuala's Moonage Daydream was just one big free parking lot. Further down the main street were the popular shops like the supermarket, newsagent's and dry cleaner's.

Nuala continued stocking shelves in loose white jeans and shapeless grey tee shirt. She was thinking of the guy from Barbados. Nuala loved his green eyes: they were strong. As if they'd already seen everything. He was young, attractive and his expression was one of cynical potency.

She walked back behind the counter. It was such a fluke that he'd stumbled into Nuala's Moonage Daydream looking for milk. Nah, she thought, there's no such thing as coincidence. We don't know what to call it so we call it coincidence. I'll check my cards tonight.

Someone was crossing the road. It was Andrew. With

hands in loose trouser pockets, black jacket unbuttoned and flapping in the light wind, he looked magisterial as he sauntered towards Nuala's Moonage Daydream. The palm of his hand slammed against the glass door and it swung open. He kept coming. Nuala looked up from behind the counter and beamed.

"You never said you were working today," he stated.

"Oh." Nuala inched her sharp red fringe and ordinary blue eyes closer to Andrew's face. "What do you want?"

"I got another letter."

"What? When? Today? Impossible."

"It was left in our porch. I didn't get up till eleven and there it was. You didn't –"

"Nope. There was nothing there. Definitely nothing. Oh Jesus, it's Saturday . . . that means it was hand-delivered." Nuala rounded the counter and placed her hands on Andrew's shoulders.

"Nuala, this is getting to me. They were in our estate. Past the gates –"

"Don't let it get to you. Come on, Andrew. They're just trying to get under your skin. Don't let them . . . remember the simple fact that some sad bastard doesn't like you. It's just work-related. What did it say?"

"*You're dead* – the usual." He stared past her to the cash register.

"Yeah, well just relax and wait. They'll slip up and then we'll know who it is. *Then* we'll strike. We'll sue that fucker. Get him fired. Whatever takes our fancy." She bent over to scoop a plastic wrapper from the ground. Her shoulders hung before her waist and her head stared upside-down between her spread legs and out the window. Her body was clearly an equal partner to her brain. She heard Andrew swallow. She swung upwards and her head whipped by Andrew's face. Her cheeks were flushed, as she announced loud and clear, "Don't let the fuckers get to you. You're getting *me* nervous now."

Andrew walked to the window and pressed his high forehead against the glass. Nuala followed him and took a firm grip on his elbow and turned him around. She searched for her splenetic voice and found it. "The fact is, Andrew, this guy could be out there. Ten thousand miles away, squatting on the moon and staring off into space. You *need* to be more paranoid. But not silly. And sweating and having panic-attacks *is* being silly. Just keep your eyes open. Listen to the most mundane things people say to you and finally . . . you'll know who it is. Trust me."

"Yeah, you're right. Gotta go . . . I'm meant to be at the club."

He nodded his farewell and Nuala nodded her grunt. She felt a premature excitement: the type that made children stammer before the big ride even began.

Shane pulled up onto the pavement in his silver Puma and jammed up the handbrake. Beside him on the passenger seat was a box of Terry's chocolates and a single red rose. That should definitely do the trick, he thought. To show her how sorry he was for being such a complete wanker that morning. He held the car phone in his hand and aimed the sun's reflection from its metal edges towards the second O of Moonage and traced it. He decided to keep Patrick talking until he got to E. "No, man, I don't believe you. There's no way you completed *Resident Evil IV* without cheat codes. I can hear a magazine in the background. Bet ya you're browsing through a games mag right now as we speak."

"No, Shane, I'm sorting through the new frame booklet," a south-side accent exclaimed. "Someone's got to run the business."

Hieronymus Bosch, Shane's art print shop in the middle of Dublin's most exclusive mall, was open and still thriving under the stewardship of Patrick, his partner and friend from college. Shane hadn't clocked into Hieronymus Bosch since the day before he went to Barbados. That day, Shane had stood in the middle of his spacious shop and scanned the walls lined with metal-framed print hangings. The main wall was arranged with assorted layman crowd-pleasers by Sandro Botticelli, Dali, Schiele, Van Gogh and Picasso. They all meant nothing to Shane. Unlike the two smaller walls where a collection of his personal favourites hung: several Rembrandts, *The Annunciation* by Martine and Memmi, a very singular van Eyck and his absolute pet, *The Kitchen Maid* by Jan Vermeer. But recently all art just looked like more art.

"Frame booklet," Shane guffawed. "Like fuck. Go on, read what you're reading."

On the other end of the line there was a pause, punctuated by a deep inhalation. "OK . . . last week some genius broke the record for the world's fastest French fries."

Who is that fucking prick? Shane thought. Through the front window of Nuala's Moonage Daydream, Shane could see Nuala with her hands on another guy's shoulders. They were talking. Intimately.

"Yeah?" Shane had to struggle to control his breathing. "How did he do that?" That fucking *cunt*, Shane thought, has just left Nuala's Moonage Daydream.

"He made an enormous bazooka from a drainpipe, which fired a potato at 250 kilometres per hour through a tennis racket strung with titanium wire and – well, that's it – the world's fastest French fries."

Where is that stupid fuck going? Shane thought. This way. Shit. Shane watched him cross the road. He was broad and well dressed in a spruce dark suit. He opened the door of his black BMW like a Hollywood bodyguard.

"So, Shane, when are you coming back in? It's sort of difficult by myself. You know? And Orla was on the phone and –"

"Patrick, can't hear you. You're breaking up, man." Shane hung up and turned the ignition. He pulled off without indicating or checking his mirrors. "Bastard, bastard, *fucking* bastard," Shane muttered as his rival drove into the light traffic two cars ahead of him.

Shane followed the black BMW deeper into the heart of a tree-lined wealthy suburban neighbourhood. He didn't know the area but liked the look of it. There were lots of big houses, kaleidoscopic in colour and shape that were perfect for big families. It was the type of area that you could walk alone in at night.

I should just take 'no' for an answer, Shane reprimanded himself. Because that's what her boyfriend is – an obvious metaphor meaning 'unavailable'. I should be in work with Patrick instead of sitting in my car with chocolates and a fucking red rose. Shane closed his eyes and mentally summoned Nuala's twisting, turning, body-parts. He opened his eyes and shouted, "Fuck!" before jamming on the breaks. Inches separated the car-bumper and the pale pedestrian. Beyond the zebra crossing the BMW was pulling in. Shane did the same.

The narrow street was lined with shops ranging from beauticians and barbers to fashion boutiques and butchers. The BMW was parked three cars in front. Its door swung open. On second viewing, the boyfriend appeared even more handsome. He looked about thirty and super-fit. As he walked away, he seemed tall, erect and rather sophisticated. He disappeared into a building.

Shane slammed the door, bleeped the alarm and smiled at the sound as if it were the technological bugle of awaiting reinforcements. He walked the short distance, turned and observed the polished glass-front of the Tone'n'Health Club. The huge window was soundproofed and it felt bogus being so close to the pumping metal weights and the dancing troupe of sweating men, yet hearing nothing but the noise of burning fossil fuel behind him.

Shane took a deep breath and wrung the tension from his fingers. He opened the door to the din of metal industry and grunting workout. The gym was about thirty square feet, centred by an aerobics dance floor and bordered by mirrors. The high treble of bubble-gum pop belted from speakers. There was no sign of the boyfriend.

"Hell-ooh, what can we do for you?" He was a middle-aged skinny man dressed in an orange tracksuit. He was bald except for a rim of white hair fitting onto the back of his skull like a silken horseshoe. He stood behind a desk and held a live phone away from his head. Shane often wondered why it was a fact of life that people with pointed noses always ended up holding authority over everyone else.

"Twenty Marlborough, please."

"Oh, a comedian. Hey, it's all right. I'm Frank. Want to join? No big deal. Some people are shy about it. But no matter what shape you think you're in, there's always someone else on a running machine near you in a worse condition. You'll see. Anyway, you look in OK shape for a boy of your age – which is what? Twenty . . . four?" Frank smiled and raised his white eyebrows. "What are you? Let me guess . . . a mature student?"

"Business*man*."

"Hey, Sylvester," Frank hollered above the music and sweat production. "I've got a live one here. Cover while I hook him up and fry him."

Shane was bent over a bike dressed in a pair of black shorts and a white tee shirt. He had no trainers, just flip-flops. The sorry outfit was a 30-minute loan from Tone'n'Health Club. Beneath the tee shirt small pads were attached to his chest and connected by wire to a beeping heart monitor.

He'd spotted his rival: skipping about twenty feet away on the periphery of the aerobics floor. He was dressed in a tight white tee shirt and black skin-tight bicycle shorts. His bronze waxed thighs flexed perfectly each time the rope whipped by beneath his feet. His leg, neck and arm muscles expanded and contracted as testicle-like pistons punched the internal flaxen walls of the skin. It was as if his ancestors had invented lithe.

Shane shook his head to free beads of sweat clinging to his eyebrows. He cycled faster and faster until his face looked as if it would implode. He imagined crossing the aerobics floor and kicking that polished fucker in the balls.

Blackness invaded the rim of Shane's vision. Pins and needles twinkled down his arms. His pulse pounded in his temple.

"Oh my God," Frank said. "In relation to your youth, height and weight – according to this machine, you're dead. But looking at you – you're in great physical shape . . . of the flesh like." Frank stood back and nodded his smirk.

"I'm going to . . . get sick."

Shane was showered, dressed and was fixing his hair in the wall-length mirror. A row of blow-driers rested on a shelf and he thought that a nice touch for a man's gym. "Here's the membership forms, Shane." It was Frank. Quickly Shane scanned the first sheet, found the annual fee and muttered, "Jesus," before handing the forms back unsigned.

Outside it was getting dark. The summer suburban skyline was purple and ensnared with wires, power-lines and flashing signal transmitters. He grunted at the BMW as he passed it by. The car was new and shiny. Shane jammed his key into the door of the Puma and noticed the *boyfriend* walking on the far side of the street, his black jacket open with flaps blowing in the wind like a slow-motion action hero. He turned and disappeared into the murky hole of a public toilet.

Shane sat into his car and clicked on the radio. He changed the channel. He changed it again and again. He checked his watch. He checked the dashboard clock. He opened the car door and began walking down the street. Shane increased velocity and dodged between two moving cars. Inhaling a lungful of something like fresh air, he entered the bunker-like toilet. The tiled floor was slimy with moist grime. There were five vacant urinals and three washhand basins. Two of the mirrors were cracked from the centre due to the impact of something like a forehead. The caged strip lighting was an uncomfortable glare. Outside he heard a cyclist zoom past with a smooth clicking sound.

I couldn't have lost him, Shane thought. He turned and examined the five cubicles. Four doors were open and one was shut. There was a shuffling sound. Then a strangled groan and a muttered, "Good boy, clean it up. That's it, clean it all up."

Shane felt stranded. He quickly stepped into the next cubicle and pressed himself against the wooden divider. There was graffiti all over the walls and Shane scanned the multicoloured scribbles for a band he actually liked. Then he glanced at his watch. It was getting late.

"Yeah, all right, see ya, Andy. Enjoy the weekend."

Shane listened to two sets of footsteps smack against the wet floor. When there was silence he stepped forward from the cubicle and felt magical as if he'd just come alive from the wall.

"Tommo?"

Shane froze.

"OK, Tom then. I'm Eddie . . . wha' bleedin' kept ya? I've been here waiting like a prick all bleedin' day." Eddie was smaller than Shane but about the same age. He was dressed in navy tracksuit bottoms and an opened plaid shirt. He moved forward from the exit with a hard-man wobble. When he was less than two feet away he looked Shane up and down like he was a possible acquisition. Eddie's cheeks glowed above a patchy black beard adorning his chin. The cheap opened plaid shirt showed off the rigidity of his pale breastplate and prominent ball of an Adam's apple that was somewhat redder than the rest of him. Eddie's face was narrow and long. The skin unblemished yet leathery and pulled too tight. His most pleasant feature was his eyes. The view of a soul. Light blue like the Renaissance eyes of Christ. "Ya don't bleedin' say very much but I suppose yer all right lookin'. Andy didn't tell me that but pity the rest of your club mates don't look as bleedin' good'n' hard as you. Andy said youze did this all the time – why are ya so bleedin' rattled?"

"Do what all the time?" Shane swallowed.

"I know what youze bleedin' boys like but." Eddie threw his arm around Shane's shoulder. "Andy told me 'bout youze."

Shane nodded and forced himself to smile. Eddie returned his smile and nodded downwards. "Go on then, look at me prick."

Oh shit, Shane thought and lowered his head. His eyes widened at the gorged instrument protruding over Eddie's tracksuit-bottomed waist elastic.

"Like a bleedin' baby's arm holding a bleedin' apple!" His arm was still draped over Shane's shoulder. Shane felt the grip tighten as Eddie's face contorted as if he was heaving a rope. Suddenly a spray of golden liquid arced from the erect penis and into the air before streaming down against the white marble of the urinal.

"Jesus," Shane said and his voice echoed.

"Yeah," Eddie said and grinned as his cock continued to balance its fountain without digital support. "Look at dat – I'm bleedin' gifted, I am. I can even piss while me cock is hard."

"Your mother must be proud," Shane said and shrugged off Eddie's draped arm.

The arc of urine lost its strength and lowered to the tiled floor until it died in a trickle and finally a last gasp droplet.

"Jayzus, Andy told me dat's your bleedin' ting – what's da story with ya, Tony?"

"Look, man," Shane said as he reached into his jacket and probed for his wallet. "For thir – *twenty* quid tell me about Andy. How you know him and for how long has he –" There was a white light. A burning heat and falling. Shane's life caught cold. There was nothing left but a shiver. His legs didn't exist. The back of Shane's head ricocheted off the tiles but it didn't hurt. It was his upper lip that stung. And the salt taste. A swinging boot excavated his stomach. A brief spurt of Coca-Cola filled his mouth. He stared up at his attacker: a pencil-line moustache, short hair split to the side, wings of a plaid shirt divided by rows of ribs and an X-ray breastplate. Malnourished yet athletic. Shane imagined force-feeding Eddie's head to the street and down a drain with the grills still intact: like some sort of sewer mincer.

"Do u tink I'm bleedin' stupit? Tink I'm a bleedin' nabber or someting? I'll tell ya fuck all, ya copper cunt!"

"Scumbag," Shane muttered from the ground while rubbing the side of his face. "Scumbag poxy fairy."

"Bleedin' copper bastard! One minute yer Tom, then next yer some prick called Tony? I'll tell ya what ya are, ya wanker, yer bleedin' garda filth – dat's what yer are but." It was all feet. Eddie swinging his runners against Shane's kneecaps, thighs and buttocks, as if his body consisted of rugby balls tied together with strings of molecules. Shane rolled with an agility he didn't know he possessed and lunged from the sitting position back onto his feet. But just as quick two arms wrapped around his neck and his attacker squeezed against him like a threatening germ on a potential cadaver.

Shane remembered the fight he'd indulged in after the soccer international. There had been a moment of disturbance. The clear-cut chance to end things early. The bobbing Union Jack-painted face. Guard down. His own fist clenched. But at the final moment there was always the fear that his foe would hit him back just as hard.

But this time Shane shoved back his elbow without hesitation. There was a crack. A glob of thick nasal blood splattered from Eddie's face to take oval shape on the tiled floor. It was a vision so foul that it cleared the air. Eddie slipped and his head collided against a washhand basin and he crumpled to the wet floor with a moan. He tried to clean his nose but just smeared his sleeve with blood and rubbed the rest into his brown moustache. For a second Shane was fascinated at how a person's innards could be made public. Eddie's mouth hung open and Shane stared at the teeth. The only part of the skeleton exposed. His knuckles smacked into the side of Eddie's face and he heard the teeth crack and splinter. The jaw seemed to dislocate itself with a click and a tooth hanging by a red thread rolled out of his mouth. Shane's knuckles burned and it felt good in a way that people don't know what's good until they've had a bit of bad. Shane took a step back and looked at the remains. The blood, the ridiculous moustache, the grease – Shane imagined Eddie shitting through his pores.

Shane bent down to the pulverised face and wiped the blood on his hand against the flap of the plaid shirt. Then he took a step back and kicked Eddie in the stomach.

Outside, night had fallen. Someone else was approaching – a middle-aged man in a suit with a gym bag thrown over his shoulder. His jowls hung like the curse of the rich.

"Tom?" Shane said as the man entered the public toilet.

"Yes?" Tom stopped.

"Wife and kids keeping well?" Shane asked without looking back.

"Em . . . yes . . ."

Chapter Five

Andrew's kitchen was painted white, had designer blinds and a varnished parquet floor. The electrical appliances were modern, white, and flashed their blue digital readouts. Everything was clean and edges of cold steel coruscated beneath the strong spots fastened to sturdy wooden beams across the high ceiling.

"How do I look?" Andrew asked. He wore a black tee shirt, black jacket and black jeans.

"Good, cool, whatever," Nuala said with a cigarette in her mouth as she hurried by in a red bathrobe to click on the kettle.

"C'mon, Nuala, no smoking down here. How do I look?"

Nuala took a final deep intake, held her breath and opened the window. Then with a whooshing sound she blew a funnel of smoke into the patch of back garden. She flicked the butt out and shut the window.

"One more time." Andrew checked his watch. "How do I look?"

"Nice."

"Nice?"

"Yes. Nice."

"Perfect."

Nuala shook her head. "No, you don't understand. Nice is for girls that aren't pretty and for boys who want to get laid by those same girls."

"True, but it's Matt and the office crowd. Must put in an appearance 'cause I missed the last two. Sheila wants you to come."

Nuala, who had been pouring coffee, banged down the plastic kettle. "You never said." She grabbed a spoon and noisily stirred. "I need advance warning." She poured the milk and splashed some onto the spotless white counter. "I'm *not* going."

Andrew fought against the urge to rush for the kitchen roll. "I know, I know . . . Jesus. See ya."

"Hold on." Nuala sort of skidded across the kitchen in her fluffy red slippers. She reached out and with her forefinger removed a blotch of shaving foam from behind his right ear. "There. *Now* you're perfect. But be careful. You know, one day you're going to be in the wrong place with Matt and the rest and one of your bent boys is going to come over and say more than hello. And then you'll have a lot more to worry about besides the prick who's sending you these letters."

"I don't care about the letters any more." Andrew felt the five yellow envelopes folded in his jacket pocket pulse against his chest. Relax, he told himself. Paranoia. But so what? There's no such thing as paranoia. There's only self-awareness. He swallowed and jammed his fingers into his jeans to stop them doing something suspicious. "As long as

I look OK – as long as I look like it's soooooo great to be straight."

All through the fifteen-minute taxi ride to the city centre, Andrew sat in the back seat re-reading the letter that had been left in his porch that morning. The font was the usual: antiquated and typed on a manual typewriter.

By the time you've read this, I will have stood outside your little dollhouse. I will have walked by your big black car and looked through its windows. There will probably be a book in the back seat. Wildlife, nature, that sort of thing.

I'm now back from standing in your porch. There *is* a book in the back seat. You're so fucking easy. What's it like knowing that your killer was standing on your little patch of land? I saw you last night. All alone with your books. I bet you thought about Berlin. I bet you thought about the things you did. Reading with the lamp on damages your eyes. I'm going to damage your eyes. You worked out hard at the gym. You always work out hard at the gym. Your muscles and health won't save you. I think I'll kill you when you're just walking down the street. Or in a crowd. Just walk by. Knife you with a neat spike. Keep walking. Maybe Matt and Sheila and the others will be there. Maybe I am Matt or Sheila or one of the others. Maybe I'm all of them. I can read your fucking thoughts. I don't like them. I'll butcher them too.

Andrew got out at George's Street and gladly passed by his old haunts, the Globe and the George, before bisecting Grafton Street and its throngs of tourists and marauding traveller children. Buskers strummed Oasis while teenage boys decked out in last season's Top Man vomited their Big Macs outside Burger King. A ten-minute stroll brought him past St Stephen's Green to the POD. There was a queue and Andrew reluctantly joined it. A few years ago he would have just skipped it with a pat on the bouncer's back.

"Regulars only. C'mon, forget it. Fuck off, not a chance. Regulars only . . . Andy. Jazus, long time."

"Hey." He couldn't remember the bouncer's name. They all looked the same. Tight hair. Coked eyes. A gait of utter derision for the living. He climbed the metal turret-like stairs, paid his money and enjoyed the trip down the catwalk entrance as a spotlight trounced its way through dry ice and hardcore techno to illuminate new arrivals. Liam was as usual sitting up in the DJ booth.

"Hey you, radio up to Liam for me."

The bouncer, a carbon of his colleagues outside, cocked his head to one side and said, "Fuck you." He pressed a finger into Andrew's chest. "What are *you* on?"

"Liam." Andrew peeled a twenty from his back pocket and handed it over. "Radio him. Tell him Andy's here."

Three minutes later Andrew and Liam were alone in the packed sweaty nightclub. The old stone alcove was arched and a fat red candle flickered on their table.

"Jessy T – up and coming." Liam nodded towards the DJ booth suspended fifteen feet above the throbbing flesh floor. His brown hair was receding but cut short and tight in a futile effort to disguise it. His blue eyes were lined and a little shadowed with bags but a perfect complement to a pale face. He wore a black denim shirt and loose black cotton trousers. Black boots added a few inches to an average frame.

"So you run Saturday nights now?" Andrew waved away

the floating smoke. He was sure he'd had this exact same conversation the last time he'd seen Liam – about two years ago.

"Every fortnight. Every other Saturday we're at the Kitchen. Got Coxy secured for next week. Want a pass?"

"Nah, my ballroom days are over."

Liam laughed instead of doing what Andrew wanted – which was bow his head at his old boyfriend's profusion of ascendancy. Liam embarrassed Andrew. He was the type of guy who had tried everything and liked everything by the time he was twenty-five. But now Liam was thirty-one. He should have a career. Or at least *own* a club.

"Hey, Andy, it's really great to see you. Really. Such a long time. How are things? You're keeping well? You look it anyway."

"So-so," Andrew said and yawned. He was sure Liam was now dyeing his hair. The music was too loud and he hadn't heard half of what Liam had said. He reached for his breast pocket. "There's a problem."

Suddenly Liam kissed him. Andrew tasted curry. Liam's tongue was wet and fat and pounding into his mouth like the hot living thing it was. Liam mashed his crotch against Andrew's leg and trapped him against the old stone wall of what was once a CIE bus depot.

Andrew shoved him away and snapped, "What's the matter with you?" He dried his mouth against the back of his hand.

"God, I'm sorry." Liam ran his hands over his hair and stared into the candle on the table. Then his eyes widened with a bright idea and he placed a small white pill on the table before Andrew's block of folded arms. "A Mitsubishi. For old times . . ."

"There's a problem." Andrew placed his forefinger on the pill and shoved it aside. He dropped five yellow envelopes onto the table. "Someone knows."

Liam scanned the packed dance floor. "Knows what?"

"Berlin."

Liam stared at Andrew. "Fuck."

The glare of the study lamp seemed to suck up the smoke and leave the rest of the darkened room clean and healthy. Nuala cleared her throat and knew the room wasn't healthy. She flicked her red fringe and leaned into the screen to type to Batfink.

<Supergirl> al right Batfink so you like fun and games in the open air – you're shaping up nicely to my criteria. Let's see if you can pass the final test.

<Batfink> hitme.

<Supergirl> you're a gamey dude – would you be with another man?

Her fingers pondered the cigarette tips nestling in the white box and decided on a specific one. Outside the window and across the street a full moon hovered above a neighbour's slated roof. It reminded her of the holy Host. She looked at the screen again and tutted.

<Supergirl> Jesus Batfink of course it's sex I'm talking about. You failed the test. You're not who I'm searching for. You're surplus to requirements.

<Batfink> Come on Supergirl. Don't do this to me. Please. I was enjoying this. Come on.

Nuala covered her mouse with the ball of her hand and clicked 'disconnect'. The modem hung up and Nuala liked the snap-sound. It was final, ruthless and everything the steel chip nightmare of technarchy should be. Nuala checked her watch. Two-thirty on Sunday morning. She stood up and walked to the window. "You still there?"

The fox was on the other side of the neatly flowered road. It sniffed at a neighbour's black bin-bag, which was stuffed with cut grass. Nuala pulled her red dressinggown tighter around her. Three houses down and parked on the other side of the road was a red sports Mercedes. She could see the red tip of a cigarette brighten and then fade. "Glad I'm not paranoid," she muttered.

* * *

Twelve years ago Nuala was already broad-shouldered and round-breasted for a sixteen-year-old. Her hair was thick and naturally black with a straight ordinary fringe.

Nuala lay belly down across her bed. She was dressed in loose pink pyjamas. Her mother had bought them in Brussels. She liked the way the pyjamas were airy and light, especially when the wind blew the rain against the window and everything in the world just seemed perfectly snug.

A black Sony tower system took up the corner of the room. Rested on the glass turntable lid was a portable CD player wired to the back of the stereo.

She dangled her battered paperback copy of *Narziss and Goldmund* to the thick woollen carpet as a Kate Bush song moped from the speakers. Nuala looked up and saw her father standing at the half-opened door. His shoulder rested on the frame and his hand balanced a glass of white wine.

"Dad, you're going to have to knock. You gave me a fright." Nuala stretched from the bed and reeled in the novel. She looked back to her father. He hadn't moved. A deep yellow cardigan was buttoned over a growing belly that had hosted far too many long lunches in Europe. His once-dark hair was rapidly thinning and almost totally grey. It both impressed and dismayed Nuala that she could remember his black hair. It was the cash-for-favour scandal that did it. Stole ten years of his life in six months. Nuala didn't know much about it, as it was never spoken of in the house. Though she'd tried to keep abreast of the story but each time she'd opened the paper the photographs of her dad's frightened face being hauled before the tribunal just made her crumple it closed. He hadn't been the main guy. He had just been one of the guys. A minister had to resign but her dad managed to stay on board whatever high-flying advisory role he played in Europe.

"Well, Dad . . . what?"

He moved his wineglass in circular motions and swirled the Chardonnay about. He looked past her, over her head and down the spine of her pink pyjamas. Nuala wondered if they reminded him of something.

"Oh nothing. Nothing, Noodles. Just tired from the flight." These days his deep but soft voice was permanently hoarse. It was the perfect soundtrack to his drooped eyes.

"The week before Christmas you're bringing me shopping in Brussels as well as Mam. Aren't you?" The trip was already organised but her father's face just craved attention without having the ability to ask for it.

"Yep, Noodles. Brussels won't know what hit it."

"Cool."

Her father raised the glass to his mouth and, although his lips didn't part, the wine mark rapidly lowered. He then smiled into the desolateness of the glass and dragged the door shut behind him.

Nuala rolled onto her back. It will be weird when Dad's dead, she thought. She could sort of see it in his eyes. A cloud of absurdity.

Suddenly the door swung open. A woman in her mid-forties kept walking. Bleached blonde, cream Valentino suit and perfect make-up. She was a busy mother: combining her florist shop, which was really a hobby, with being the perfect host and housewife.

"What?" Nuala sat up.

"'What?' she says. What! I know you let *him* back into the house. You were seen. Jesus Christ, Nuala, he's a – he's not welcome here."

Nuala raised her eyes and tutted. "Andrew's still my brother. Just because you and –"

"He's no longer our son. I told you. I explained to you. What else do I have to do to make you understand . . . how could you?"

Nuala disguised her smirk with a pretend yawn. That afternoon she'd let Andrew into the house so he could browse through her new CDs and see which ones he wanted to borrow. It had been the first time he'd been home since their parents threw him out a month ago. It had less to do with religion and everything to do with morals.

"Yeah, well, he just wanted some CDs."

"CDs?" Her mother placed her hands on Valentino hips and glowered. Then she sighed and spoke softly. "I know it's difficult for you, Noodles. It's difficult for all of us. Andrew – Andrew just let us all down. But he can change if he wants to. He just has to decide. Your father knows a doctor who can help him. But it's up to Andrew to decide. You really shouldn't have gone and betrayed us like that, Noodles. Do you know how disappointed your father is?"

"Dad knows?"

"My God, he's terribly upset with you. We *trusted* you." Her mother shook her head dolefully and left the room.

"Bitch," Nuala muttered. Her dad mildly unnerved her. What's he up to? Nuala thought. He was getting weirder and weirder since the scandal. *The* scandal. Besides her gripe with the papers it had never embarrassed her. In fact it had made Nuala feel special. Teachers had taken her aside and under the obvious guise of concern grilled her about Dad and home and Dad.

God, he looks old, she thought. Way more than the decade he has on Mam. I wonder what he feels each time they get trapped together in their bedroom's big mirror. If I were him, I'd feel that she was stealing my years. It's meant to be a partnership.

Three weeks later Nuala lay belly down on the thick white rug beside the flaming gas fire. Her folded arms acted as rest-stool for her chin. Beside Nuala and sitting on his winged high-back leather chair was her father. A coffee table supported his Waterford crystal whiskey decanter, which had been a gift from the Tánaiste. A pair of 1950's-era brown-framed reading glasses balanced on the tip of his nose. In his lap was a leather notepad, which he'd been hunched over for the past two hours. His gold pen moved like a chisel as if writing to him was artful Morse code.

"How can you sit there for two hours and just write," Nuala mumbled from above her crumpled comfortable chin.

Her father replied without looking up from his notepad.

"I just sit here and ask a stupid question and keep asking it."

"Oh," Nuala replied and she didn't look away from the television. Though she did say to herself: come back, come back, come back. She was sick of her dad being weird. She was drained of all sympathy. Now she just saw it as some horrible weakness – as if a person only loses control when they're hiding from the past *and* afraid of the future.

That night Nuala couldn't sleep. She opened her eyes, closed them and opened them again. Was there something she'd forgotten to pack? Was the alarm set? Passport left out on the dressing-table? No, yes, yes.

The door creaked. Someone entered the room. Lying on her side she blinked to the red glow of the radio alarm clock. One in the morning. Was it Mam? No. Nuala could hear her below still click-clacking across the kitchen tiles. It had to be Dad.

He was respiring above her bed. Deep bass tones that made her picture his dark forest of nasal hair. His breathing remained deep and steady.

Pretend to wake. Stay asleep. Pretend to wake. Stay asleep.

A large palm cupped her forehead and barely squeezed. His fingers ran down her back. She knew he was trying to be gentle but he was too big and old and his fingers too clumsy. Nuala stared at the clock's digital read-out. She didn't know what it read or how many minutes had ticked away. Her mind rocketed through a million irrelevant thoughts until she realised that her continent was the only one not to begin with the letter "A".

He kissed her cheek. A simple, dry, quick peck as if he was an amateur collector of responses.

"Dad . . ." She was surprised at hearing her own voice and at how rational it sounded.

"Noodles," his hoarse voice whispered.

Nuala heard her pulse loud and clear and was certain that the room, house and perhaps the world vibrated with it. The red glow from the digital read-out was still a blur and things raced through her mind as if she were trying to perfect the theory of everything. He was gone. She knew that. No deep breathing.

Two hours passed and the digital read-out blurred in and out of focus. Her arm was dead and she wanted to change position but she was paralysed.

Suddenly there was a rap of knuckles against the door. "Nuala," her mother whispered as the door softly opened.

"What, Mam?" Nuala sat up against her pillows and squinted against the rectangle of light pouring onto the carpet from the landing. Her mother's hair was invisible beneath the curlers and clips while a heavy red dressing-gown enveloped her proud shape.

"It's your father . . . I can't find him."

"Haven't seen him." She bit her lip.

"God, Nuala, wake up. I'm worried. He's not in the house. I mean he *was* in the house an hour ago when I went to bed. He was pottering. But he never came to bed. And now he's gone . . . will you get up? *Please*, Nuala."

"Yeah, yeah, yeah."

Her mothered disappeared and Nuala put on a purple silk dressinggown. She took it off. Quickly she wriggled out of her pink pyjamas and kicked them under the bed. Then she put the gown back on.

"Dad, come out, come out, wherever you are," she muttered while her bare feet padded across the landing. Something hit her on the head. It was wet and warm. Nuala touched her hair and looked up. "Jesus, I don't believe this," she muttered.

Something was leaking in the attic. A steady stream of drips squeezed between the attic lid and plopped to the carpet.

"Mam," Nuala called down the stairs and startled the house with normal volume, "you won't believe this. A pipe's burst."

Mother and daughter gathered beneath the attic hatch and stared upwards.

"Nuala, you go up and see what you can see."

"Why me?"

"You know I hate the dark."

"What about your son and heir? Opps, I forgot. You threw him out. Silly me."

"Oh Christ, go on, Nuala, please."

Nuala poked at the attic hatch with an iron pole before pulling down the wooden steps. The attic floor was boarded and once at the top Nuala remembered her bare feet.

"Shit, where's that switch." She felt her toes absorb a shallow pool of warm water. She found the switch drilled into a central timber beam and flicked it on. The attic was so filthy it had its own ecosystem. Corners of beams and roof padding were home to dark spiders in fluffy webs and the side concrete wall was being slowly colonised by creeping moss.

Nuala turned and stared into her father's face. His tanned skin had turned pale as if he had a skin under his skin. He was hanging from a central rafter, his neck preposterously narrowed by twisting rugged twine. His brown slacks were dark with a urine stain and Nuala gagged as the sudden stench went so far up the back of her nose that it was a taste and not a smell.

"Dad," she whispered and lowered herself onto her knees.

The police and emergency services arrived to a state of general calm. Nuala's mother was pale, trembling and sitting downstairs on the sofa. She didn't seem to grasp what had happened so she kept asking, "What happened?"

Nuala led the way to the attic. When they cut him down they fucked up and let her father fall through the attic hole and onto the bright landing with a thud. He fell like nobody. Not like a Kennedy or a Gandhi. Nuala was leaning against her bedroom door, watching everything and trying to figure out where Dad could possibly have gone.

* * *

Nuala clicked off the lamp and exited the computer room. Her bedroom was next door. Without turning on the light she lay down on her single bed. She felt like scratching her face. Itching her legs. Stretching out her arms and twirling around. A wish for take-off. An inclination to explode. Instead she untied the dressinggown. The flaps fell back and her breasts melted into her body. She wore expensive red knickers. Most of her lingerie was exorbitant and intended for the appreciation of two. But Nuala had bought them simply because she liked to spoil herself. Her slippers fell to the floor with a light thud.

* * *

Shane stood over the toilet bowl pissing. Wind chimes hung from the window and a dozen of Lisa's Body Shop jars were still spread across metal shelves. He listened to the toilet bowl and thought how consummate, how computer-like the draining penis was. "Libra," he muttered. "Dimples distinguish the

Libra." He earmarked the page of the paperback *Sun Sign Secrets* and dropped it to the floor. It suddenly occurred to him that Lisa would have loved Nuala's Moonage Daydream. He didn't wash his hands. That was something he only did in restaurants, bars, anywhere in the company of witnesses.

Shane strolled into the living-room and past Patrick who was blowing into his mug of coffee. Patrick was heavy and usually wore brown. His life was imprinted on his twenty-three year old face: dull, pliant and already lined. His brown hair was shaggy and thick and every four months plucked at by a barber. He had narrow lips and watery brown eyes. He wore shapeless brown cords, a v-neck navy jumper and a vest underneath. Patrick had never got to grips with fashion. He just didn't know how to dress himself. His shoes were old black slip-ons. His faded denim jacket was in a pile on the sofa beside him. A rolled *PC Games* magazine peeped out of its pocket.

Shane walked over to the huge bay window, which overlooked the Liffey. His forehead suctioned itself to the cool glass. Throngs of students and tourists squeezed across the Ha'penny Bridge and Shane wondered how there were enough nightclubs and bars to cater for each one of them.

He returned to the sofa and lifted his own steaming mug from the coffee table. "OK, Patrick, you've had an *excellent* idea." He nodded at his friend and lowered himself onto a lumpy red beanbag.

Patrick smiled and cleared his throat. "Like I said, it's just an idea. Nothing more. But it's a good one." Patrick inhaled and then loudly exhaled.

"Yeah, what is it?" Shane wasn't interested in talking shop. Sometimes he wished he needed employment for more important things than just to oar through the passage of time.

"OK, well, last Saturday when I was standing on the side of the road watching the marathon –"

"Standing on the side of the . . ." Shane incredulously muttered. "Jesus."

"And a runner was wearing some video store's tee shirt saying, '*It's the first world. Don't invent it. Don't create it. Just rent it!*'"

"I'm lost." Shane tipped his ash.

"So I thought," Patrick continued, "we should *rent* framed prints as well as *sell* them. No one owns his or her city centre apartment any more. I mean, look at our places – with our rents neither of us will ever save enough for a down payment on a mortgage. So renting is the future. And people can rent a print frame for – one year, two years and change them whenever the *mise-en-scène* of the art world changes."

"*Mise-en-scène?*" Shane laughed. "You just said *mise-en-scène*! That means you're gay. Either that or you're spending far too much time on the phone with Orla."

"Orla's our bread and butter, bud," Patrick admonished.

"Look, Orla may be our bread and butter but she's also a fucking halfwit." Shane stood up, kicked aside the beanbag and pulled over a seat from the dining-table. "Look, things are working nicely the way they are. So why change? I sort of like the idea of year zero. Maybe in the future or something."

"I'm finding it hard to give a shit when you don't," Patrick muttered and made a wanking gesture with his fist. His forehead was always sticky. He nodded into Shane's open-arched kitchen where a dreary brownish print of James Abbot McNeill Whistler's ageing mother hung above the white rarely used cooker. "Haven't noticed that before. So much for your abandoned thesis – *Abstraction is a French-fried philosophy*."

"That picture is there because I like *it*, not the movement." In the last few days Shane had noticed his appetite for art return. It was as if an old broken watch had suddenly started ticking again. It was nice. "Look, Patrick, talking shop is a bit sad at the best of times, never mind on a Saturday night. I mean, Jesus, I may as well hang a banner outside my window – 'Wankers of the World Unite'. Now, while you were busy doing things like standing on the side of the road looking at Johnny-no-mates jog by, people like me were doing interesting things like kicking the shit out of junkies in public toilets."

"No way." Patrick sat forward. "Go on."

Shane told a story about deciding to take a piss and being hopped on by a junkie. It was an exorcism of that mule-like human being. The rent boy had the unforgettable look of an animal at the bottom of the food chain living out its last skinny days of illness. His image was graffiti on Shane's brain.

"Nice one," Patrick said. "But you could always handle yourself. Me – I don't think I could hurt anyone. Not in real life. Not even in that situation. I don't know whether I'd freeze or just think, 'Well if I don't resist it'll be over faster'. And if I did hurt him . . . like you did. Hurt him bad. Then I think I'd feel pretty bad too." Patrick wiped his forehead and red streaks remained across the flesh before quickly fading.

"Feel bad? Jesus, *fuck* him. When I think of that cunt I just get that feeling like – like he's a person who I would never *ever* enter a burning building for. And I feel bad about *that*. Since then I've been noticing people I've never noticed before. Well, *rarely* noticed before. I'm not just talking about the down-and-outs. But everyday people. And they're everywhere. Behind the counters, driving buses, digging roads, even in the fucking cops. But I don't notice them because – because we only notice our own kind. Imagine Patrick – imagine never *ever* being worth a girl's second thought." Shane observed Patrick's deep glow and his averted eyes. He knew he shouldn't have said that. Patrick was his best friend and business partner. But sometimes – sometimes he just *asked for it*.

Patrick sipped his coffee. He always sipped because he didn't like to drink. Finally Patrick looked up and said, "I just want you to know that you seem – you seem to be pulling it together after Lisa. Poor Lisa. Sometimes I still can't believe . . . well, you know."

The heaviness returned to Shane's stomach. Sometimes he pictured it as a grey thick cloud, swirling around and dirtying his insides. Other times he saw it as a black anchor. He remembered the very last time he'd seen Lisa. Beautiful in a coffin. Beautiful in a light white dress. Shane reckoned that putting dead people in clothes proves what great thinkers we are. It's the most brilliantly obscure solution of what to do with our dead. Shane had touched her hard cold forehead and inhaled through his nose. He'd wanted to catch the scent of death yet he knew that there was no such thing. Decay and rot are just the smells of infinitesimal life forms teeming. The only scent Shane had caught was of roses. Red roses.

Shane shrugged and lit up another cigarette. There was

very little left of Lisa in his realm any more. He'd never been close to her work and social circles and now they lived in an entirely different world.

"Shit," Patrick said. "Sorry for dragging it up. Shouldn't have said anything. Did I tell you I reached level nine?"

"Level nine?" Shane nodded his commendation.

"Without cheat codes. The Dungeon Master's a lunatic – he needs eight *direct* rocket hits to take out."

Shane checked his watch. Almost midnight. Worse time of the week. Midnight at home on a warm Saturday night. He wished Patrick would go. "Um . . . sorry man. I'm completely wiped. Keep it till tomorrow." Shane stood up and gestured towards the hallway and the lovers' lantern. Patrick checked his watch and feigned surprise at the time. Shane led the way into the hall and they both flexed their shoulders against the sudden awkwardness.

"Oh yeah," Shane said as he opened the door, "got myself a new girlfriend."

Patrick stood back and looked Shane up and down with exaggerated awe. "What's she like? Why didn't you tell me? Jesus, Shane."

"Just someone I sort of met in Barbados. Met her again by accident the other day."

"What did I tell you about that trip? Knew it was the thing to do. Come on, what's she like?"

"Let's just see where it goes. Wish me luck though."

With a rare alacrity Patrick stated, "You don't need luck, bud." Then his shoulders quickly drooped and he was gone.

Shane walked back into the living-room and over to his full library wall. He ran his finger along a dozen spines. Lisa would have reminded him to ring his father that afternoon.

But since the funeral Shane couldn't bring himself to do so. "Walk tall," his hunched crooked father had told him at the top of the church and Shane had replied, "It's hard to walk tall when you're at the lowest point in your life, *Dad*."

Chapter Six

It was Sunday evening and children were playing on the road. Packs of them. They used the pretty tiled speed bumps to launch their luminous mountain bikes into the air. They wore vinegary crash helmets. When Andrew was their age there was no such thing as a bicycle helmet. It was in his late teens that they'd first made an appearance and even then only utter wankers wore them. Everything's fucked up in the twenty-first century, he thought. Everything's judicious.

Andrew had always been queer. He'd never gone through a phase of even wanting to be heterosexual. In his pre-teens he didn't mind the company of girls – unlike his more macho playmates. But he'd never been feminine. His favourite game with the boys was six-scrap – a complicated game where six boys would wrestle each other all afternoon until it was time for tea. Andrew zoomed through his cosmopolitan adolescence with ease. He'd had the odd girlfriend to keep the pretence up and even forced himself to finger-bash the more demanding ones in the corrugated shed of the local football pitch.

There's something wrong when there's even a responsibility to rape, Andrew thought. Use a blue pill. There's a pill for everything. There used to be even one for Liam. The Mitsubishi. A nice white little thing. Waves of warmth beginning in Andrew's head, fisting down his throat, glowing through his innards, pulsing through his parapet erection and mating against the twitching servomechanism of Liam's sphincter muscle. Liam had been so perfect once. Now he was just a sad joke.

There was a small pedestrian gate beside the huge electronic ones. Andrew twisted his key and stepped outside. I don't want to see Liam again, Andrew decided. I wish I'd left him in Berlin. Berlin had been an escape. Berlin had been an escape downwards. Now it's Sunday night. Warm and stale. A summer's evening. Everything is serene and hushed and paused. And when nothing happens it's just crisis catching its breath.

The local bar was OK. Old men, some in caps, nudging their lips to their Guinness. Happy types of style-less middle-aged couples sitting against the counter, looking up at television and occasionally offering each other the word. Younger couples or threesomes or foursomes took the tables and talked low about another week. The pub was grey, with white lamps on the walls. There were photographs of the pub from a hundred years ago. It hadn't changed.

Andrew walked through the narrow lounge and passed two tables of bored elbows and shrugged conversation. He pushed open the toilet door and centred himself at the grubby open-winged urinal. Another man followed and positioned himself to Andrew's right.

A packet of cigarettes landed on Andrew's shoe and

came to rest half on the murky tile and half against his heel.

"Shit, my back's at me today. Could you pick that up?"

Andrew said, "Sure," and zipped himself. He crouched towards the cigarettes. A black shirt drifted by Andrew's eyes. It covered a flat chest that rose and fell like a hospital respirator. The bottom three buttons of the shirt were undone and the parted flaps revealed a belly-button which was a dark cavity crowning a spreading river of light brown hair, which quickly darkened to a black pubic bush. He didn't seem to be wearing shorts and his cock was only an inch from Andrew's face. Andrew swallowed. It seemed semi-erect. Despite pointing to the floor the blue veins were alert and poised for sudden movement. The foreskin had rolled back of its own accord and the smooth shining head was pink and polished.

"Here," Andrew said and handed him the packet. He observed his own left shoulder while speaking as if that would hide his redness.

"Thanks."

Quickly Andrew claimed the only handbasin and began to scrub his hands. Damn, damn, he thought, I didn't even look at his face. Not even his face. God, I'm getting old.

There was a gust of wind and the noise of the flapping door. Mr Perfect Cock hadn't washed his hands. He was gone, faceless and ageless, and that's about as exciting as the Cavern has ever got in its entire history.

Andrew steadied the door open. Where to sit and read *Cetacean* magazine while sipping something not yet decided? Only two tables left.

A man standing beside the cigarette machine smiled at Andrew, then waved. It suddenly clicked – black shirt. He was fidgeting with his Discman's earphone connection as if wanting to make a technological insinuation. Something like, I have a Discman so I'm just here for the quaint value of superannuated holes.

Andrew walked over and said, "Em . . . yeah?"

* * *

<Supergirl> that's why I'm tense. Death threats. I'm going to go insane soon. My life is killing me. Everyday stuff.

<HornyDub> Jesus and you're not making this up?

<Supergirl> no.

Nuala adjusted her study lamp to illuminate the flat of the desk beside the purring computer. Six gold-plated Tarot cards were laid out in the shape of a cross. Beside them another four rested in a horizontal line. The remainder of the deck was neatly piled beside her elbow. Fuck, she thought, The Seven of Wands. Incoming . . . Judgement. Big yawn. End result . . . The Tower. Lightning, frightening.

<HornyDub> So Supergirl, like my pic?

Nuala summoned his picture with a click. A nice blond nineteen-year-old boy. She reckoned the picture was a fake. She couldn't imagine a gorgeous libidinous bronco living in uncivil Coolock. Up there they put speed bumps on the road to slow stolen cars, not to protect children from their parents' new Jaguars.

<Supergirl> Yes.

<HornyDub> Gonna meet me? In the wilds of nature like you commanded. And remember, I like men too.

<Supergirl> Maybe. You seem to be exactly what I've been looking for.

<HornyDub> You're gonna meet me and find yourself. And we'll have a crazy time. What is the pursuit of sanity but madness?

<Supergirl> Very poetic, rough boy.

<HornyDub> Stop calling me rough. I'm nice, snobby girl.

<Supergirl> Nice? Fuck nice. Nice is boring.

<HornyDub> Those threats are definitely getting to you.

<Supergirl> You are nice. Why else would a rough boy work for Amnesty? But it blinds you, stuck in there surrounded by all those other nice people. This is the 21st century. People care about what they're told to care about. It's like South Africa: there's two things people hated about it – apartheid and the niggers.

Nuala inhaled her cigarette. Andrew was back from the Cavern. She could hear the key turn and the door open. Someone was with him. Murmurs. Shit, she thought, let it not be that insufferable fat prick, Matt. What was Matt doing in the Cavern?

<HornyDub>Jesus, supergirl. You don't believe that?

<Supergirl> Of course not. And it's Supergirl. With a capital "S". Don't piss me off about it.

Footsteps on the stairs. Nuala pulled tight her heavy red dressinggown and tucked the lower parting between her knees.

<HornyDub> Sorry, SUPERGIRL. Didn't mean to hurt your feelings. Sensitive, aren't we?

<Supergirl> Of course I'm sensitive. I am woman. My only education is my heart. Hold on like a good rough stableboy.

There was a knock on the door. "Enter," she said and immediately turned off the monitor. There was a click followed by the applause of static.

"I'm back."

"Uh-huh. Who's here?" Nuala inhaled the cigarette and watched her breath dim the light. She thought of her lungs and entrails. She pressed her elbows against her sides as if her organs were trying to escape.

"The most amazing guy in the world," Andrew loudly whispered. "Turn around, Nuala."

Nuala turned around. "The most amazing guy in the world? You met *him* at the Cavern? What is the most amazing guy in the world doing in a place that looks like the insides of someone's liver?"

"Keep telling you, Nuala: get out there. Greet life with a smile. Even on a crappy Sunday suburban evening. Look at me with Mr. Perfect-straight-but-a-fag-virgin downstairs on my sofa wanting to know what the view's like on the other side."

"No way." She stood up and smiled at Andrew. She liked him when he was very happy. It meant he had a reason to be happy. The rest of the time Andrew seemed happy for no reason and that, not infrequently, irritated her.

"Suppose I'll just have to tell him about the other side. Better yet, show him."

"Disgusting," Nuala said with a smirk.

"Be nice, little sis." Andrew leaned forward as if his voice wouldn't carry without a nudge from his face.

"I'll get nice when I get ugly."

"Look, we need some privacy, so . . . you know the drill."

The light from the landing fell on Andrew, and Nuala fathomed just how handsome her brother was. Such a strong face, deep eyes and thick, *thick* black hair. He was so lucky with his hair.

Andrew left the room and Nuala sniffed the air. His aftershave lingered. Calvin Klein: such a straight aftershave.

Nuala turned the monitor back on and skimmed the screen.

<HornyDub> Supergirl?

<HornyDub> Supergirl?

<HornyDub> SUPERGIRL?

<HornyDub> Fuck sake. SUPERGIRL!!!!!!

<HornyDub> !!!!!!!!!!!

Nuala started to type.

<Supergirl> Relax, sweetheart rough boy. Tomorrow. Two fifteen. Sit by the pond. Centre bench. Don't get that wrong cause there's only three benches and that would be a disappointing endorsement of your intelligence. Bye, bye. XXX

She waited for the reply.

<HornyDub> XXXXXXXX slobber, slobber etceteras.

Nuala snapped her mouse over 'disconnect'. A moment later she was descending the stairs, making sure her red slippers made no sound. Outside the living-room she flexed her hand above the gold ornamented handle. She remembered the last time she'd barged in. It had been about three on a Sunday morning and Andrew had brought home some gorgeous eighteen-year-old from The George. The three of them had had coffee and then Nuala had gone to bed. But ten minutes later she'd charged in with something like, "Anyone see my pen?" The guys had been snuggled together on the black leather sofa. The younger guy's fist had been a blur and Andrew's penis thankfully invisible as if it were a cybernetic rotating blade protruding from his spread Versace legs.

Nuala rapped her knuckles against the white gloss paint while simultaneously turning the handle. "Coo-eey, just me," she said and shuddered at the thought of being in the devil's heaven.

She marched into the bright living-room. Blazing, she thought, blazing. Where are the shadows? Music was playing in the background. Trance chill-out crap that Andrew hadn't played in months. Nuala glanced at the television. Blank screen. "Andrew?"

Andrew was sitting in the centre of the three-seat sofa leaning forward with elbows propped on his knees and his chin supported by cupped palms.

"Where is –"

"There." Andrew peeled one finger away from his chin and feebly pointed in her direction.

Nuala looked behind the door.

Shane sat awkwardly in the black leather chair. His index fingers touched and made a flesh triangle before his face. He swallowed. He was trying to be cocky.

Give it ten seconds, Nuala thought. See what happens. Don't spill the beans. My big brother could kill him anyway.

"I'm Shane," Shane said. "Pleased to meet you."

Nuala was careful not to sound too bouncy-normal-the-world-is-a-gas. She faked a half-yawn combined with cracking her fingers. She liked doing both at once. It was an excuse not to cover her mouth. When she'd finished yawning and cracking, Shane was cryptically red. He looked like a schoolboy when embarrassed. Nuala saw just fear – the anxiety of knowing that one is totally unprepared for what will *definitely* happen in the next three seconds.

Shane put out his hand and Nuala took it and poised herself for a hearty squeeze. Instead she let it drop and took her place beside Andrew on the sofa.

"So what's going on, boys?" Nuala asked while flapping over the lower wings of her warm red gown, making sure it covered her knees.

"Nothing," Andrew half-sighed and half-snapped.

"Well, not to worry. I'm here now. So what are we talking about?"

"Absolutely nothing," Andrew said and sighed again. He still couldn't bring himself to raise his chin off his pillared hands. He was glaring at Shane.

Nuala stood up. "What's Lenny doing down from the mantelpiece?" She pointed an accusing finger to the tarantula in the glass case resting at Shane's feet.

"Oh s-s-sorry," Shane said and quickly picked it up. He held the glass box before his face and shook it. "Just looking . . . like checking it out."

Nuala crossed the room and squatted down. She said, "Lenny's not dead," and softly rubbed her little finger against the front of the glass. "Lenny's alive. Picked him up in New Orleans this summer. Stopped over for two nights on the way to Barbados. Ever been to Barbados?"

Shane went redder and shook the box again. "But he is dead."

"I went to see the house from *Interview with the Vampire*. Real southern-belles-type a place. Sitting, swinging on the porch beneath a blue sky and swaying branches. It was gorgeous. Bit too hot though. Anyway, there was a dirt patch in front of me – you know, where the grass was too burnt to live. That's where Lenny and me met for the first time. He came scuttling out of the drainpipe beneath the porch."

Shane moved his thumb, centimetre by centimetre, towards her little finger on the glass cover. "Bet you screamed."

"No, she didn't," Andrew said with a snort. "I've heard this story a million times, I know it off by heart."

"Well, I haven't heard it once," Shane said and his eyes darted as if he'd said something out of place.

Nuala smiled into the glass case. "OK. So Lenny ran out of the pipe and across the dirt patch. Suddenly in front of him a kind of trapdoor opens. About the size of a Coke-can lid – crusty clay is thrown aside and out pops this fucking horrible – and I mean *horrible* wasp. It was so fucking huge. Half the size of my – no. Half the size of *your* fist." For a moment Nuala engulfed Shane's fist beneath both hands and squeezed. "So this big black wasp with thick yellow stripes hovers up about a foot in the air and lands on poor Lenny. They start fighting. I mean kicking the absolute shit out of each other. Rolling around, hairy spider legs kicking, the wasp's stick-like legs clasping and just like that . . . it's over. Poor Lenny is still. Not moving. D. E. A. D."

"Told you," Shane said and turned away to take a deep slug from the wine glass on the small coffee table beside him. Then, too quickly, he replaced his thumb beside Nuala's finger on the cover of the glass box.

"Or is he?" Nuala smirked.

"Oh, get on with the bloody thing," Andrew muttered from the sofa.

"OK. The horrible wasp starts pulling poor Lenny's big hairy body towards the hole in the ground. He gets as far as the hole when I suddenly get a strange feeling . . . like I've got to save this dead spider. So I got this feeling and I save Lenny by squishing the wasp and picking up poor Lenny."

"So Lenny is dead," Shane said. He took a deep breath and quickly added, "And I was right."

"Back at the hotel I was telling the concierge about what had happened. And would you believe that he was some kind of nature-science-student-type-of-guy. Real ugly swotty face, glasses, freckles, Mr Logic, you know? So he explains that the wasp – incidentally called the Tarantula Hawk wasp – was pulling Lenny back to its nest where it was then going to inject its eggs into Lenny's chubby body."

"So what? He's dead," Shane said.

"No. You're missing the point, ninny. Lenny is just paralysed. He knows and feels exactly what's happening. *Everything* – the eggs being injected into him, then hatching inside of him and finally the larvae eating him slowly to death over the span of *three* months. Lenny would be alive through it all. See, tarantulas go for a year without eating. He's paralysed but aware and that, according to Mr Logic, my New Orleans concierge, is generally accepted by naturalists to be the most horrendous death on the planet, crafted by nature's hand . . . or if you prefer, God, herself."

"How do you know he's still alive?" Shane asked.

"He'll fall apart within a couple of days of him being dead. Don't worry, I grilled Mr Logic on how to keep my new pet."

"Your pet is slowly starving to death and you're going to watch this for a year?" Shane circled the empty wine glass before his face.

"Lenny owes me *big*." Nuala walked back to the sofa and sat down beside Andrew. "I've pissed you off, Andrew, haven't I? I should be in bed and out of the way. Don't worry, I'm off now."

Andrew snorted.

"You sound like a farmyard animal," said Nuala. "You're doing that a lot tonight."

"Stay, why don't you," Andrew said and waved a

dismissive hand towards Shane. "Nothing's happening anyway."

Nuala raised her finger in the air as if she'd just reached an original conclusion. "Something's not right in this room. Why am I the only one with a hard-on?"

Shane went red. Andrew didn't. Instead Andrew sat forward and said, "Don't act so blasé, Nuala. Decadence to you was a condom before you moved in here. Now, back to the point at hand – Shane is a little wanker."

"Fuck you," Shane snapped before blinking with the shock of hearing his own voice. He swallowed, took a deep breath and added, "Why don't you stop talking for a minute and give your asshole a rest."

"Nasty, nasty. Be nice boys," Nuala said.

Andrew pointed at Shane. "You already admitted that you're a wanker. Just before *she* came down."

"*At the Cavern*," Shane said becoming more animated. "I admitted I was a wanker *at the Cavern*. It doesn't mean that I'm an actual wanker. Otherwise you might as well argue that – that since I was walking, I am therefore a walk." Shane's redness had spread to his forehead.

Andrew threw his arms over the backrest, spreading himself, making himself larger, more powerful, as if the opposition would find it impossible to imagine him being awkward. Nuala knew him like the back of her hand.

Andrew stood up. His face was a series of creases. "I'm wrecked. I've a busy day tomorrow. So goodnight, Nuala . . . and Shawn."

"Shane," Shane said. "Shane as in . . . Shane."

"Whatever," Andrew replied and closed the door behind him.

Nuala looked at the door. She wished its four white panels were computer screens. The Internet was *her* time. She replied only when she was ready. She could say whatever she wanted and there were seldom remonstrations.

"Well, now I've seen it all," Shane said as he rose from his seat. "I mean there's kinky shit and there's – there's just sicko people. And you guys are sickos."

"What are you talking about?" Nuala said.

"What am I talking about? Not only is your boyfriend an arse-bandit but you let him pick people up at your local boozer. Look at me – I'd spent all day trying to figure out how to worm my way into this place and in the end all I had to do was flutter my eyelids at Mr Workout Man and, bingo, I'm invited home for –"

"He's not my boyfriend. He's my big brother, you big thick . . . Jesus. Ugh!"

"Oh." Shane's arms that had been extended in animation suddenly sank by his sides.

Nuala observed his height. He was about an inch smaller than she was. "Why didn't you watch a movie? That's usually his thing."

"We did," Shane muttered before lowering his head and running a hand through his tightly cut hair. "It was a gay porno. Never saw one of those before and I've seen a lot of things."

"Oh, you're not a little boy. You're *a man* of the world."

"Didn't mean it like that." Shane crouched before her. "I meant that I've seen a lot of *straight* por- . . . shit. Too much information."

Nuala could hear him exhale through his nose. The warm air hit her chin. She sniffed and there was no odour.

"I think I pissed off your brother," Shane said. His voice was becoming more intimate with their isolation. The trance CD had ended and the lack of music brought a chill to the room.

"Andrew's pissed with any boy he can't sleep with . . . no, that's not fair . . . just *good-looking* boys he can't sleep with." She stared into his eyes. Green eyes. Swirling green eyes.

"When I told him the movie was filthy – filthy in a bad way," Shane said with an abrupt smirk, "he tried to explain how pornographers are just nice liberals who aren't so nice any more."

"Good old Andrew." Nuala laughed and placed her hands behind her head. "Full of good lines." She was aware that her left kneecap was showing through the split in her nightgown. She wanted to cover it but couldn't determine a gracious manoeuvre.

"You two are very close," Shane said.

"We're comfortable enough – or bored enough to eat in silence. A modern-day fairy-tale – except we're brother and sister."

"Let's go on a date." Shane placed a hand over her exposed knee. Nuala waited for him to squeeze and was scared that she might jump. He didn't squeeze and the weight of his hand faded to nothing.

"Most people would think you're too young for me. I mean, how old are you?"

"Twenty-three. And you've got to admit we need to know more about each other. Come on, Nuala . . . I run a successful business." He suddenly looked confused as if trying to figure out just what point he was trying to make.

Nuala leaned forward and Shane immediately retracted his crouched upper body from her personal space. His hand vanished from her knee.

"Andrew may be queer," she whispered, "but he isn't a poof. He could kill you with a single blow. And that blow would be struck with a single word from me . . . therefore I can kill you with a single blow . . . I mean, word." Nuala flicked her fringe and wished it were longer rather than being just jagged. "So don't get weird on me."

Shane smiled and Nuala realised that it was his first genuine smile of the night. His nose slightly reddened which in turn seemed to exacerbate his youth. He was watching her lips and Nuala felt self-conscious. She hoped they didn't look dry and chipped. Quickly she licked them.

"Intacta," Shane whispered.

"What?"

"Intacta."

"And I said '*what*'?"

"Nothing. Just bullshit I made up to impress you." Then he kissed her. It was a hard kiss but not clumsy. Just enough to suck her mind clean. Nuala closed her eyes. Then she opened them again. Suddenly she was overcome with practical considerations – as if she were a traveller after missing her connection. When had she last showered, brushed her teeth? What underwear was she wearing? Were the tiny skin plates of her forehead half the size of Shane's? They'd better be.

"You've got to go now," she said. "Move – on your feet, soldier. Up and out."

"What about that date?" Shane asked while grunting to his feet. "We need to know each other."

"You're in lust with me," Nuala said as she too stood up and double-tied the knot in her gown. "I just want you to know that I know it. I'm not a liddle-biddy-doodly-woodly-girlie, you know?"

Shane extracted a business card from his jacket pocket and handed it to her. "My numbers – home, work, car and mobile. No E-mail thing. Hate computers, love their games. Call me?"

"I'll *investigate* you first." Nuala liked the way they were the same height when she wore slippers.

"Investigate me?"

"Yes, investigate you. Duh. Now shoo – go on, shoo." Nuala opened the door and Shane walked by into the hall.

The front door clicked open and then clicked closed. Nuala scratched her chin and thought, so is this what it's like to be really wanted by someone you really want too?

Chapter Seven

Andrew rocked back and forth in his big blue chair. The computer hummed in the middle of his perfectly trim but expansive desk and beside the opened door, located on top of the filing cabinet, an old fan whirred. Matt was behind him, sitting on the window ledge overlooking Grafton Street. He was a well built thirty-something with receding hair but escalating energy. Moist patches darkened his white shirt over each of his recently acquired tits and Andrew was glad Matt's jacket hid his armpits from the world.

Matt stretched his foot to poke the back of the blue chair and Andrew's head quivered with vibration. "Those balloons for Mary's party, the ones Sheila blew in the photocopying room . . . they didn't survive the acupuncture treatment."

Andrew rubbed his eyes and muttered, "You're a dead man." He cautiously observed Matt as he rounded the desk to flop his bulk on the opposite chair.

"Anyway," Matt continued, "I got an invite to the corporate box on Sunday aft–"

"Croke Park," Andrew said with a sigh and leaned back into his chair. "I love big match day in Croke Park." One night an eighteen-year-old Andrew had been rigorously wanking over a picture of a Gaelic football star. A study lamp was precariously balanced on the pillow beside him. It had been in the *Sunday World* sports section. A colour tabloid photograph beneath the bold headline, *Disgraceful Scenes in Croker*. The player was lying on the grass, muscular legs spread, face contorted in agony and three opposing players glaring dispassionately down. Andrew's legs had tensed, his pummelling arm had tensed, his free hand groped in advance for a tissue. But his fingers missed the toilet roll and instead groped the lamp's naked bulb. "Fuck'n' Jesus!" he'd roared and his hand shot backwards and smacked himself in the nose. "Fuck'n Christ!" he'd moaned as a smattering of dark blood rained across his white sheets. The bedroom door opened and his mother exclaimed, "Andrew, your nose!" Then she looked some more, went red and muttered, "Jesus Christ."

"Thank God the Dubs are back," Matt said with a click of his fingers.

"Yeah, they're looking good," Andrew said.

"What the hell's that?"

An extraordinary noise sounded from down the corridor. People were speaking at a volume that was not shouting, but certainly too high for the colonnades of an office block. "Excuse me," a woman's voice caustically stated. "Do you have an appointment?"

"Jesus," a man's voice replied. "What is this place, the fucking Pentagon?"

Andrew breathed into his hands. Matt pulled himself to

his feet and faced the door with hands on huge hips like a fat friendly sheriff.

Liam rounded the corner, his lined blue eyes ablaze like a reluctant Grecian sacrifice. “There you are, man,” he said and for a second smiled before crisis once again swarmed his features.

“I’ll get security,” Matt said and snapped the phone from beside Andrew’s shock of folded arms.

Andrew placed his finger on the tone button and looked up into Matt’s moist red face. “I know him. It’s all right.”

“Oh,” was all Matt could manage.

Liam looked like a mortified schoolboy’s very dapper uncle in a grey Xebo Urbanware anorak, grey camouflage combats and red New Rock buckle boots. He smiled while stabbing his white-filtered mint-flavoured cigarette into the monogrammed sand of the free-standing ashtray. Andrew groaned. That sand had been undisturbed since the day it had been deposited into his office.

Two pairs of eyes watched Andrew. He inhaled and ran his fingers through his thick black hair. He flexed his jaw muscles and felt them indent their impression onto his cheeks. “OK,” Andrew said. “I’ll see Liam now.”

“*Liam?*” Matt said and sniffed.

Andrew stood up, rounded his desk and with his back to Liam, silently mouthed, “Fam-illll-eee”. He subtly tapped his forefinger against the side of his temple and nodded his *you-know-what-I-mean* expression.

Matt sympathetically nodded and backed out into the corridor. “Nose to the grindstone,” he said in a brave effort to revive a miscarried normality. “Speed is God, time the devil – so says Dave Hancock.”

Andrew closed the door.

"Who is that uptight fat bitch?" Liam asked as he plonked onto the seat that was still warm from Matt's buttocks. He was still frantic within his new immobility. His fingers flickered amongst themselves as if typing air while his tongue kept reappearing to water-parched red lips.

Andrew lowered himself onto his big blue office chair. "How can I put this?" Andrew's fingers formed a tense triangle before his face. "Why are you here? Why, why, why? And what are you on? It's nine-thirty on a Monday morning and you're in my office stoned on a class A drug and you're . . . you're a *fucking* poof!"

For a moment Liam found sobriety. He'd rarely heard Andrew curse outside of a sex-act. "I can't deal with it, man," Liam said, inhaled and was once again suffocated by whatever pill or powder was still working his system. "Walking home last night along Wicklow Street and don't know where or how or where or how but it was fucking there. A cop van. Back doors pop open. Pricks said nothing – three of them – took me down to Store Street. Me! To Store Street! And, man, I fucking *knew* the heat was on. But they waited instead. Got a doctor to examine me. They kept me till just an hour ago – told me they're watching me and then told me to piss off. They're onto us, man. This is it. We are so –" Liam stared at the wall. Andrew turned to observe the new object of Liam's fascination. It was just a framed quote given to him by his boss, Big John McGivern, last Christmas.

You can reach one solution in an hour, a better one in a day, a better one still in a week, but the best one, never! – EDWARD DE BONO.

Liam snorted from his intense gaze and said, "What *the fuck* have U2 got to do with this place?"

"Pay attention, Liam," Andrew said and snapped his fingers across the desk. "What are you on?"

"I lost the Kitchen deal. Raided too many times and the management reckons it's because the filth have been watching me for a year. Started a new night at the Life Bar. Down-market, full of tracksuit-knacks out of their tits on yaba – but it pays the piper."

"Pay attention." Andrew spoke very slowly. "*What are you on?*"

"Some pills . . . washed down with gin. Coming down so did some snow. Needed it . . . things on my mind."

"Things on your mind?" Andrew whispered. "Berlin . . . Kreuzberg 36?" How he despised Liam's dyed brown hair, dry lips and the tawny pools surrounding his blue eyes.

"Shhhhh," Liam whispered, "for fuck's sake, Andy."

"So the cops have been watching your pathetic minor drug dealing for the last year. Then finally, on a quiet Sunday night, they pull you in when you're out of your brain and paranoid. They then intimidate you at the cop-shop for the entire night because they've nothing else to do . . . without once mentioning Berlin and finally they throw you out. Think Liam. *Think*."

"No, you think, Andy. You weren't –"

"*Think!*" Andrew's fist smashed onto the flat of his desk.

Beneath his dark stubble Liam's pale cheeks slowly turned red. "I think I'm coming down," he muttered to his knees. "Shit, I'm so sorry. I've made an idiot of myself again. Every time I meet you . . ." Liam stood up and walked towards the door. His chin seemed glued to his chest between the spread furry flaps of his anorak. Andrew followed him and reeled him in by the hood. Liam staggered backwards and into the much more physical protrusion that was Andrew.

"Liam – if you ever – *ever* – do this to me again then I'll – then –"

"Yeah. I know, man. I know." Liam disappeared out the door and down the corridor. Andrew walked over to the window and stared outside. Telling Liam was not sharing the problem, he thought. It was multiplying it.

There was a knock on the door.

"Yep."

Matt's head squeezed through the crack. "He's gone?"

"Yep."

"Good – I mean – Nuala's here to see you." Matt withdrew his head and shouted, "Nuala! Big brother will see you now."

* * *

"'*Big brother* will see *me* now'?" Nuala said as they marched down the pedestrian side street, arm-in-arm, cutting out a short cut to the city's most up-market mall. "Yeah right. Huh, *I'll* see *you*, more like. God, and Matt's skin is so crap and leathery. I can't believe he's the same age as you." Nuala was wearing her full-length brown leather coat with cream fluffy collar. She referred to it as her *famous brown raincoat*. Peeping out beneath the coat were the black fully rounded platform heels of her leather knee-high boots. *Shit-kickers*, she called them. Nuala also wore a black peaked baseball cap, dipped quite low over her broad forehead and she somehow made it all seem cutting edge. "Can't believe I missed that pathetic old bum-chum of yours. Jesus! A coked-out paranoid faggot raving in *your* office in full view of the prime-time idiots. Jesus, I can't believe I missed that. Said that already though."

Andrew had calmed down. Nuala couldn't have timed her visit better. Later, he would explain that Nuala had known that their disturbed cousin/nephew/whatever had been making a beeline to see him. Hence his sister's rare appearance at the office. "This is crazy, Nuala. I mean if he's interested he can call me. He knows where I live."

Nuala unhooked his arm, raised an opened cigarette box to her lips and sucked one out. "Dowp be sug ah pick."

"What?"

Nuala lit her cigarette and removed it from her lips with gloved fingers. "*I said*, don't be such a prick."

"I'm not. He made it clear he wasn't interested."

"Andrew, he stayed for an hour after you went to bed, blabbing about you . . . just you. And since I'm the best sister in the world, I listened and listened and *Jesus*, did I listen." Nuala stopped again, this time to dig out blue shades from her coat pocket. She slipped the shades on, inhaled her cigarette and marched on. Andrew had to jog to catch up. "Anyway," she continued, "Shane felt terrible. He was just worried . . . didn't want to go too fast. But he thinks you're the bees-knees. And don't worry, I said all the right things . . . like promise to escort you down."

"Oh yeah," Andrew said, "like you convinced him that the only difference between homo and hetero is just a few inches in the dark."

Nuala shrieked a chuckle. "That's disgusting! All you bent-boys are *so* rude."

"If you're so good at matchmaking," Andrew began while managing to link her arm again, "then why have you never had a boyfriend?"

"Don't be silly – women prefer no sex to bad sex."

"But . . . you've had neither."

Nuala shrugged. Andrew did too. Up ahead was the shopping mall. It was just an unspectacular gold archway leading into a maze of bright corridors lined with shops selling designer furniture, jewellery and watches, imported carpets and rugs and some beauticians. There was also a small Body Shop and Nuala stuck out her pink tongue while passing the window. They turned the corner and an old-world hanging sign heralded Hieronymus Bosch.

"This is crazy." Andrew stopped and pulled his arm free from Nuala's tightening grip.

Nuala made a cluck-cluck sound and moved her elbows in and out. "Don't be such a big-girl-chicken-type-of-guy. Live by my philosophy – *dance as if nobody's watching*."

Andrew's jaw dropped. He sometimes wondered what type of magical-mystery-world his sister lived in. As far as he was concerned, he'd never met a more introverted and subtly eccentric creature than Nuala. She had few friends and besides tending to the needs of Nuala's Moonage Daydream, she rarely went out.

Andrew pushed open the door to Hieronymus Bosch. The simple wooden swing door belied the shop's impressive interior. Spacious and broad, even the multitude of framed prints covering almost every inch of wall failed to suppress the expansive sentiment. Hieronymus Bosch was about thirty feet by thirty feet with a high flat roof speckled with white spotlights. Two rows of racks, gripping clear-plastic-covered prints, lined the floor. A huge desk separated a broad shaggy-haired young man and his telephone conversation from the rest of the shop. Upon seeing Andrew and Nuala, his voice lowered to a sly mutter.

"Leave this to me," Nuala whispered as if they were in a gallery.

"Leave what to –"

But Nuala was already gone, marching between the racks of frame-less prints, up to the stretch of broad desk. "Shop! Shop!" Nuala shouted in a posh accent and banged the desk three times with her fist.

"Gotta go, Orla," the man behind the counter said and hung up. "Em . . . hello."

"Hello," Nuala said and removed her pink shades.

"Well . . . browse away. Oh and I'm Patrick. Here to help and all that." He swallowed air and lowered his eyes to the spread pages of *Bizarre* magazine. Not even the two-tone cotton single-breasted Jil Sander's suit, that said *highbrow-arts* and most definitely not *banking*, could suppress the man's aura of monotony.

Andrew approached and sniffed the air. He wished the guy would wear an aftershave. He had no odour. Andrew asked, "Shane here?"

"Shane? No. Not in weeks." Patrick sighed with suppressed umbrage. "But whatever it is, I'll take care of it."

Nuala chewed thoughtfully on her lower lip. Andrew looked at her, hoping to see some secret twitch that was intended for him only and he could then decode it and read the secret plan.

Nuala turned to Patrick and said, "Well, it's Shane we're interested in."

"Well – he's not here. He didn't say he'd be in – but then I wasn't talking to him since yesterday."

"I thought he works here?" Nuala perched the side of one buttock on the desk.

"Yeah – he used to be in and out. He does lunch with clients. You know, corporate things. Let the lawyers or accountants or brokers think they know exactly what they want, while Shane is really giving them exactly what *he* wants. That type of thing. He used to be brilliant at that type of thing."

Andrew was confused. Confused and bored. Confused, bored and disappointed. He wanted to go. Get a bite to eat and a cappuccino with a nice view over St Stephen's Green. "Is that signed?" Andrew asked. Hanging above Patrick's head was a blown-up black and white grainy photograph of an astronaut stepping from his capsule onto the moon.

"Oh yeah," Patrick said and pointed to the almost unreadable scrawl of blue ink at the bottom. "To Shane", he read, "Neil Armstrong."

"Astronauts," Nuala muttered. "Boy stuff."

Patrick laughed in a condescending way. "It's a bit more than that." Patrick lowered his eyes again and in little more than a mutter said, "It's like . . . it's like a verification of Armstrong's words. It *was* a giant leap. Their spaceship was piloted by hands and nuts and bolts. It was the last gasp of the industrial age. And with the world watching below it was 'hello' information age. That's my *aper-* that's my *aperçu*."

Andrew silently mouthed the word, "wanker," and strolled to the centre of Hieronymus Bosch. He flicked through a rack thinking, blah, blah, blah – could do better myself.

There were footsteps behind him. He looked up. Nuala was holding a postcard and broad shaggy Patrick was muttering, "It's yours. Really. You like it so keep it." Nuala was smiling and her cheeks were a slight purple and like most women she really did glow at the smallest gift.

Andrew decided to say something. He didn't like being excluded. "Why is it called such a stupid unpronounceable name?"

"What?" Nuala said. "Hieronymus Bosch?"

"Yes," he said, reddening at Nuala's perfect pronunciation.

Patrick pointed up to a hanging frame on the wall while somehow managing to keep his head lowered but his eyes raised. It contained a large murky-green print of gothic devils and gargoyles swarming around a black citadel and torturing lost souls with various ingenious instruments of torment. "*Hell* . . . by Mr Hieronymus Bosch," he said with a deep loud imperious voice that was schizophrenic against his previous comportment. "A 16th century master of stunning originality. It shocked the art world. Everyone else was still feeling like a martyr, dipping the brush into his bleeding wrists and painting the Virgin. And at the time it was still a really good idea to be a priest and accept the bribe of abstaining from sex in order to get into heaven quicker." Just as suddenly his voice lowered back to a quiet drone. "Anyway, Shane doesn't particularly like Bosch or anything. It just seemed like a good idea when we finished our Bachelor of Arts degree. Sort of chic, like . . . at the time."

Andrew squinted at the print. It reminded him of a school trip to Rome and St Peter's Basilica. A guided tour ended on a marble balcony towering above the Pope's high altar and St Peter's grave. Above was a close view of Michelangelo's painted dome. One of Andrew's classmates stared at the various explicit depictions of buggery-with-flaming-instruments and announced in a loud whisper, "That's the best shit I've seen since last summer's Wimbledon. I'm off to the jacks to have a wank".

"Now, Patrick," Nuala was saying, "when you talk to Shane make sure you tell him that we were investigating."

"Investigating?"

"Yes. *Investigating*. It's a *Friends* thing. You don't watch it?" She sucked in her cheeks until her lips resembled a kissing goldfish.

"Em . . . no."

"Didn't think so. *X-Files* is more your thing, yeah?"

"Not since the third season," he sniffed.

Andrew squeezed himself into the far corner of the elevator and spread his arms across the golden handrails. The elevator doors parted with a *ding*. Andrew stepped out and strode down the corridor. He entered his office, used a foot to pull out his big blue chair and sat down. Then he saw it. Andrew felt something die in his stomach.

On the corner of his desk was a yellow envelope. There was no address, no position title, and no stamp. It had been hand-delivered to his office – not dumped into the external or internal mailing system.

"Oh God," Andrew whispered as if just realising that things that go bump in the night are in fact entirely real. He carefully cut through the paper with his letter opener and unfolded the usual A4 page of crooked faded font.

I'll enjoy berlin I know killing you

Andrew made a decision. It was time to tell Nuala the truth.

Nuala dropped her fourteen-year-old battered yellow Fiat from fourth gear into third and the engine revved horribly. She could afford a new car but couldn't be bothered buying one. She'd never enjoyed driving and if she lived in a warmer country she'd cycle everywhere.

She careered around a corner and past the flower gardens of the huge public park. A hedge rocketed by like a green superhighway. Then the hedge fell to a wall and the wall shrank in chunks, like a giant's staircase, until the pond was visible.

The car shuddered to a halt and Nuala jammed up the handbrake. She put on her pink shades and baseball hat, got out and back-kicked the chipped yellow door shut. It was a quiet road she'd parked on. The big houses were tall and silent. Nuala had forgotten how there were still so many places in a large city devoid of humanity.

Nuala examined the park's wall. It rose to her thighs. There was a drop of about ten feet on the other side. Then there was a patch of grass, big enough for a father and son's football pitch.

Twenty yards away a solitary figure wheeled his mountain bike along the pond's circumference. An old couple flung bread at the ducks and he said something and they nodded. He parked his bike against one of the three benches and sat down on the middle one.

Nuala felt a victory-roll in her brain and it occurred to her that for such an indiscriminate waste of time, life could be quite exciting.

He was already on his feet and following the path

towards her. Nuala once again checked the height of the wall. Her heart was racing and he was closing in across the deep green grass.

"Supergirl?" He looked up from behind a red scarf.

Nuala raised her chin as if that was sign language for 'affirmative'.

He wore a heavy black jacket fastened with gold buttons and the collar turned up. A red scarf was wrapped around his neck and mouth and his face only began at his nose. He had a crew cut, which seemed a personal choice rather than a rudimentary goon must-do. And an earring! Large and round like a gypsy's. What was he, Nuala thought, a tinker, a drug addict, a burglar? The only working-class person she'd ever fraternised with was the cleaning lady.

He pulled down his scarf. They were the largest lips she'd ever seen outside of a television screen. Red, oily and always poised to be kissing life. She saw his eyes. Deep, deep blue.

So this is HornyDub, Nuala thought. And in the flesh, he is his jpeg-picture. And he's not strange and he's not dangerous. He's just the young bronco stud from Coolock.

"Well, Supergirl? Strangers when we meet?" His voice reminded Nuala of a girl she'd never liked at school. It was a voice that searched for big words it couldn't pronounce. A voice that always failed to smooth over the hoarse gravel of a reluctant working-class background.

"I don't know where . . ." Nuala began but immediately realised that she was speaking too softly. She took a deep breath and began again. "I don't know where you got that line, but it wasn't your head."

"Oh?"

"Must be a poem or crap lyric, I suppose."

With a sharp intake of air he said, "Better then 'do ya come here often?' huh?"

Nuala adjusted her pink shades beneath her baseball hat. "Good one. I just felt a twitch of the old zygomatic and orbicular muscles."

"Huh?"

"That's cracking a smile, to you."

"Supergirl, gonna give me a real name?"

"Supergirl, that's it." Nuala's attention drifted by his image and his words to the swelling blue sky pouring out of the white summer clouds far above the park's green forest. Beneath the echo of quacking ducks, tweeting birds and the distant splash of falling bread, he was talking. He'd mentioned his name. The information just floated around her. "I need you," she announced.

"Just what I wanted to hear," he said with a slut's smile.

"You've had many naughty thoughts about those woods. And I like them. But today I just wanted to see you . . . to make sure you fit the bill for my master plan. And you do. So that's cool."

"Fit the bill?" He moved forward but ceased immediately as if worried he might startle a fragile animal.

"I want you for a friend . . . out there in the woods. And then, afterwards, I'll play too. I'll e-mail you soon. See ya, HornyDub."

"But what about now?" he said. His fists were opening and closing. He couldn't contain his desperation. "You're up there. I'm down here. So close – life just isn't fair."

"I hate people who say that. I mean, just what is your basis for comparison?"

"Huh?"

"*Huh,*" she successfully mimicked, though her pink shades cost her the double-whammy of the facial expression.

Nuala sat into the car, took off her shades, turned the key and sped off. "Right on time," she muttered while checking her two-pound Casio digital watch. She slowed down while passing Nuala's Moonage Daydream and soaked up the hippy-dippy wavy sign above the grim metal shutters. The thing Nuala liked best about her shop was that it had enough interesting angles to make it renewably futile.

Nuala sped around the corners of pretty suburbia and the houses got bigger and the roads got wider and paradoxically less busy. She drove between tall redbrick pillars, which supported a pair of black electric lanterns. The driveway was gravel and Nuala loved the crunch of wealth. The house had been built in the 70's but still looked brand-new – untainted redbrick façade, large Canadian wooden window frames, double front doors and twin garages. Pine trees blocked the view from the road, not that the neighbours would find anything particularly curious about Nuala's mother – financial scandals and her father's suicide were *so* last century.

Nuala used her own key. The hall was huge and Nuala missed the space and privacy. She reckoned that one day she'd move to the midlands and buy an old mansion with the remainder of her trust fund.

"Noodles," her mother called from the kitchen.

"Yep, it's me, Mam." The door to the kitchen had a glass porthole. Nuala opened the door with a swing of her hips and marched in.

"Just in time, Noodles, kettle's boiled." She was reading the paper while sitting at a large white table that commanded the centre of the room.

"Why the long face?" Nuala asked.

"Oh . . . Jim McCarthy is dead. Remember him? He lived around the corner – always gave you and your brother chocolate and biscuits on Halloween night."

Nuala grunted. She'd prefer if her mother would titter over the obituary column rather than brood over it. It didn't suit her glamour that refused to fade with the onslaught of age. Her mother had an allure that's been there and done that. With peroxide hair, ostentatious make-up and clothes, she held the poise of a woman who had got even and therefore is entitled to enjoy a long old age.

Nuala loved the kitchen. The dishwasher and fridge were disguised by decorative teakwood panelling. Beneath all the shelves and cupboards were hidden strips of yellow lighting that made the kitchen glow with inviting heat. The cooker was huge and digital while the oven had three levels and was as tall as a freezer.

Nuala went straight to the kettle and opened the cupboard above it. Everything was always in the right place. Her mother seemed to collect things and never throw them out, as if life were some type of hobby. Nuala snorted at the still-wrapped citronella torch that rested in the corner of the cupboard behind the coffee jars. Why would anyone in Ireland need a citronella torch? she thought.

There was a stuffed bag from the local supermarket resting on the counter. Nuala stuck her nose into it in search of nothing in particular. She found it.

"What's this?" Nuala plucked a plastic bottle from the bag and carried it to the table along with her coffee. "And what's wrong with my shampoo? Full of natural stuff and all."

"I know, Noodles, I know. But this is good. Jackie begged me to try it and I did and it works."

"Jackie is a silly hairdresser, Mam. I'm a herbal-naturalist . . . mineralist. Let me see what it says on the bottle – *Fruits 2-in-1 Normal Shampoo and Conditioner. And because Fruits contains simple, trusted ingredients, it will leave your family's hair beautifully soft*." Nuala waved the bright bottle before her mother's smirk. "What are these simple trusted ingredients? *Water*, so far so good. Uh-oh! What have we here? *Sodium laureth sulfate, cocamidopropyl betaine, dimethiconol, carbomer, glycol distearate, laureth-4, DMDM hydantoin, guar hydroxypropyltrimonium chloride*." Nuala paused and raised one eyebrow at her mother. "Paying attention? Say that one after me – hydroxypropyltrimonium." Nuala caught her breath and continued. "*PPG-26, tocopheryl acetate, sodium citrate, sodium lauryl sulfate, sodium chloride, fragrance* . . . fragrance? Jesus! And last but not least the trusted, caring and simple ingredients we all know and love so well, *CI 47005* and *CI 16255*. God, Mam, I'm very disappointed."

"You're my daughter, Noodles. I made you and love you and bathed you, yet I have to admit that you are the most tedious individual I've ever had the misfortune to come across."

Their conversation briefly turned to Nuala's Moonage Daydream. Her mother was always interested because it was originally *her* florist's. After her husband had hanged himself she'd never returned to work. Nuala reckoned that bouquets and death were analogous inside her mother's head. But that wasn't so bad. Inside Nuala's head, it was urine and death.

As usual the conversation swayed uneasily onto Andrew-the-outcast's life.

"*He's* OK then?" Her mother bit her lip. The lines around her eyes warped and distorted their delineation.

"Yeah – the usual. He's a bit stressed now and then. Sign of getting somewhere in life. You don't get the pay hikes without spilling blood. Still not going to talk to him?"

"I'm not even going to talk *about* him."

"It's a bit silly, you know? He's queer, Mam. Born that way, etceteras. You're not *that* backward."

"It's your father's wish – he said he'd disown him until Andrew changed. Look, Noodles, I'm not discussing this any more. You're always bringing it up – week in, week out."

"Dad's dead and *you* brought it up." Nuala sipped loudly on her coffee. She remembered her father's corpse lying in a new suit in a new coffin in the spotless living-room packed full of other people in new suits. The Tánaiste was there and the mourners were as interested in glancing at him as they were in glancing at her dead dad. Nuala thought there was something quite humiliating about an open coffin. She imagined herself lying there. People could do whatever they wanted. Smile down and mutter their hatred. Look at her breasts while pretending to take one last soaking stare at her face. They would use her as a curiosity, a sneak preview of how, one way or another, they too would definitely end up.

Nuala remembered being in the hospital the night her father hanged himself. His two sisters were bent over the metal bed, whispering in the corpse's ear. They were uttering prayers, tagging them on as passwords to his soul to make it easier for him to get by the bouncers of heaven. Nuala had observed her aunts with withering disdain, as if it were they and not death that had overstepped the limits.

"Will you not do something about your hair?" her mother asked while flaming a cigarette and instinctively brushing a hand through her own thick groomed peroxide hair. It was a standard question that wasn't really a question – just something that was said every week. Nuala would usually laugh about dyeing it blue next and her mother would inhale into her hands as if she believed her.

"Do you think my hair is slutty?" Nuala asked, grabbing one of her mother's cigarettes. She flicked her crooked fringe and thought, I'll straighten it for Christmas, maybe before that, maybe even in time for winter.

"Slutty?" Her mother was surprised. "No. Well . . . you know what I mean."

"Do you think I sleep about?" Beneath the table Nuala's knees pressed together.

"I'm your mother. You shouldn't be asking me these things."

"C'mon, Mam. More like sisters and all that. So, do you think I sleep about?"

"I think – I *presume* you've – what's the new fangled term? *Experimented*. But 'sleeping about' is a bit more derogatory – like for girls who want their cake and eat it, yet they're the ones who get left on the shelf."

"So you think I've experimented?"

"Well, I mean, my God, who wouldn't? You're so lucky – your generation. We had to creep about . . . creep about all the time."

"So Dad . . . Dad was the only one?" Nuala rarely mentioned her father. She once overheard her mother tell a close friend that some college of science had rejected his corpse once medicine had finished with it.

Her mother's eyes lowered towards the table. "He *was*." Nuala's mother took a deep breath. "He was when I married him."

Nuala tried to say something but her face involuntarily twisted into a silent, "Huh?"

"On your honour, Nuala, you must swear – swear to God – on your poor father's soul, that you'll never repeat this to a living being."

Nuala, who neither had any honour, nor believed in God or in the poor soul of her father, swore it.

Her mother glanced at her watch as if the ordinary world would return when the big hand hit twelve. Then she said, "I had an affair. Just before your father –"

"Just before? Who?"

"Months before," her mother continued. "A brief thing. It was more for company. Christ, it *was* for company. The bed thing . . . it came as a package."

"Bed thing? Jesus," Nuala said softly. She wished Andrew were here. Then he could do the outraged-son-thing and shout and seethe and say what *should* be said.

"I'm not telling you who it was, Noodles. Some things are *real* secrets. But it's no one you know. A husband of a friend. Sounds awful, I know. But it wasn't. It was – it was company."

"Where? Where did you – just where did you?"

"A city centre hotel." Her mother covered her face and began sobbing. Nuala reached out but was shocked to realise that her mother was in fact laughing. "God, it was funny. We knew it was funny. Using different names like I was a Bond girl. Strange times."

Nuala put out her cigarette. It didn't taste nice any more. Mam had had an affair, she thought. She betrayed Dad.

She's lived a better life than I have. She's got more balls. She's not afraid. She's more – more curious. My mother is – not better than me – but *knows* more than I do.

"Are we friends?" her mother asked and smiled in an everyday way as if admitting she'd forgot to tape Nuala's favourite programme.

"Oh yeah . . . of course. God, it's cool." Nuala reached for another of her mother's cigarettes and quickly lit it as if the flame would sear the word 'cool' that still hung in the air. "I didn't know that you were unhappy with Dad."

"Unhappy with Tim? I wasn't. He – he was away. All the time. You remember? He was busy – work, work, work – and that bloody – that bloody effing tribunal had started to happen. It wasn't his fault, Nuala. You mustn't think that."

Nuala inhaled and thought, I never thought that.

Her mother continued. "His job was why we had the house and cars and dinner parties. But something happened out of the blue one day between me and – my secret. And it made sense. It made sense for some weeks until it didn't. It was nothing to anyone but us and then it was over. And – and to be honest I don't regret it. Never did."

"Yeah," Nuala said. "It's not what people say or do that matters: it's *why* they say or do it. That's what Dad said, and he was always right about everything except when he took cash for favours."

Nuala's mother laughed. "And it wasn't even a mistake on his behalf. What was it they called it?"

"Benford's Law," Nuala said dryly. "It's inexplicable. And it's not fair. It would be black magic if it wasn't suddenly *scientific*."

"Even after all this time I still don't understand," her mother said with a sigh.

"It's easy, Mam, if you concentrate." Nuala inhaled and with a gush of monotony said, "Benford's Law states that any ragbag of figures will obey the demand that 30 per cent of the numbers will start with a 1, 18 per cent with a 2, right down to just 4.6 per cent starting with a 9. After a century of being ignored – because educated people like me simply refused to believe that it could be true – computers discover that stock-market prices, census data, and even the heat capacities of chemicals obey Benford's Law."

"Still means gobbledegook to me – and how do you know all those figures? Your brain is wasted in that shop."

"Of course, the tax inquisition people learned the law and while there was nothing remotely suspicious about Dad's accounts, Benford's Law stated that they were too regular and therefore the books were cooked. Further investigation proved the law correct. I'm telling you, Mam, there's something evil about it."

"I think you've got black magic in the head," Nuala's mother said. "Those cards you do –"

"The Tarot? They're great. I learn things about people that I should never know. It's unfair but, fuck it, I want the upper hand."

"Nuala, your language."

"Sorry, Mum." Nuala looked at her mother's blue eyes. Great and blue, she thought. Mine are nothing and blue. If I didn't get her eyes then why should I get her ageing glamour? Anyway what would I do with ageing glamour?

Nuala drifted to her mother's nose. There was a light sprinkle of foundation on it. It reminded her of the Sahara's red dust that had covered both Andrew's car and her own one morning when the wind had blown it across the continent. At least I don't need foundation, Nuala thought.

"Another coffee, Noodles?"

"Another coffee . . ." Nuala felt the cold air enter her nostrils before exiting warm a second later. "Nope." She watched her mother watch her. There was a smile on her mother's face that was slowly fading. Nuala gave a happy smile, a smile that said, it's OK, I'm cool with everything. When Nuala was ten, her parents' friends would ask, "Hey, Noodles, why the long face?" "But I'm *smiling*," she'd say and sulk for the rest of the day. Finally Andrew instructed her to "Hold that face," and took her upstairs to his bedroom. "Now that," Andrew said in front of his wardrobe mirror, "is a long fucking face."

"Mam," Nuala said, "do you know what the most perfect box in the world is?"

"Em . . . no, Noodles."

"It's a shoe box. That is the most perfect box in the world. A shoe box."

"Oh yes, that's right. You made pretty jewellery boxes for children last Christmas with all those shoe boxes from town. Great seller too, weren't they?"

"Yep," Nuala said and beamed because she knew that there had never been anything in her shop that had been a great seller. "Gotta fly. Remember I'll be dropping all that stuff in. Talk to you before the weekend, Mam." Nuala stood up and made the sacred sign of the mobile across her brown painted lips with thumb and little pinkie.

"Stupid prick," Nuala muttered as she solemnly pushed the plate to the centre of the black metal table. He should have rung, she thought. He knows I can't cook. He knows I depend on him for that one thing. Bastard!

The sausages looked as if they'd been fried in hell. There were also charred rashers and a burst soggy egg. Andrew hadn't come home from work. Nuala had waited and waited before her patience had snapped. Rummaging through the fridge, she'd found bacon and other pig meat with which to destroy Andrew's pan.

Nuala couldn't focus on anything. Food, her mother's affair, television, her mother's affair, anger at Andrew's negligence, her mother's affair.

She'd changed into a purple dress she'd bought at a second-hand stall. It was encircled by red swirling patterns and was quite beautiful. It definitely didn't look second-hand. She'd told Andrew it had cost eighty pounds and he'd believed her. Nuala was also wearing one of Andrew's white shirts. He had a dozen of them.

My mother has beliefs, she thought, is a friend of God's, has principles and thoroughly believes that one day she will have to account for everything – every breath. And she was still able to do that. Mam was *fucking* another man while Dad was in Brussels, while I – while I was struggling with my faith. Hold on – I never struggled. I believed. And now my mother tells me that when I was a teenager I'd got down on my knees every night for all the wrong reasons.

Nuala grabbed the hem of her purple dress and swished it from side to side like a bored *can-can* girl. Her mother had never even asked for forgiveness. That galled Nuala. And forgiveness for what? She scratched her head. Forgiveness for living more than her daughter had lived? Forgiveness for having better stories to tell?

Her mobile was on the coffee table. She picked it up and cursor-keyed her way through its electronic phonebook until the blue digital screen lit up the name, *Stalker*. Nuala pressed the green button.

"Uh-huh," a voice said.

"Inspector Nuala here," Nuala said.

"Hold on till I swing over. Jesus, learn how to drive, *bitch* . . . you still there?"

"Yep."

"So, you investigated me – that was cool. My mate Patrick wants to sleep with you."

"Ugh – is he retarded?" Nuala paced the room.

"No. He's all right. On my way to see him now, in fact. Risk night."

"Risk night?"

"Board game. Requires skill and strategy."

Nuala lit a cigarette. She inhaled and imagined Shane on the side of the road somewhere in his little-boy-racer car. "I think you're a stalker."

"I'm not a stalker. Look, I swear I got locked in that night and then I fell asleep and the next thing I knew –"

"Drive here and wait outside." Nuala hung up.

She was about to rub her dry lips when she remembered carefully administering dark brown lipstick after her bath.

There was a noise from the back of the house. Nuala didn't like being home alone on this particular night. Too many themes in her head. Another noise – a dull thud – from the kitchen.

Nuala felt nauseous as she entered the hall. She put her hand on the kitchen door and was very aware of her own mortality. "Hey . . . em . . . Ross and Joey!" Nuala shouted.

"Come on down from upstairs. There's noise in the kitchen." She counted to three and opened the door.

Andrew was sitting at the kitchen table. His hands supported his face. "What are you shouting about?" he asked, his creased brow embellishing his mashed features.

"Fuck!" Nuala said. "I didn't know you were in. When did you get in? What are you up to?"

Andrew did that thing with his eyes that always managed to communicate a logical command. Nuala sat down.

"What am I up to?" Andrew stared at the table. "Nothing. Why?"

"Where were you? When did you get home? Why are you creeping about?" Nuala noticed her half-crumpled cigarette packet in her hand and said, "Shit".

"Jesus, Nuala, I was upstairs. Got home at the normal time." He still wouldn't look at her.

"You got home at the normal . . . what about my fucking dinner?"

"Thought you'd get takeout."

"Takeout! You know I can't have takeout. Not with all that monosodium glutamate. I'm a junk-aholic. You know that. Jesus, Andrew – want me have a relapse or something?"

"Sorry."

Nuala reached out and plucked his hand away from his chin. "There. You can look at me now. Want to know what I think? I think your life is so perfect – so smug and snug that when some asshole pokes fun at you with these poxy shitty fucking letters it can make you into the snivelling mess that you are right now. Pull yourself together, soldier, and make my dinner. Nope – don't. I made my own. But you can do the washing up – as usual. And I fucked up your pan. Ha! And how come I didn't find you – hear you even?"

Andrew didn't smile. Instead he ran his hand the wrong way through his hair before patting his thick black mane back into place. "I'm not snivelling," he said with his own disinterested sigh. "And I was upstairs. In my room. You walked right past after your shower. Jesus, Nuala, you couldn't find snow in the Arctic."

Nuala stared at Andrew. He looked older. He looked as if he was getting to that stage in his life where he should buy a little dog and wait for Mister Right to come along and then move to California.

"Andrew, cheer up." Nuala took his cheek in a pinch. "It's just a bloody letter. Someone who doesn't like you and has no balls and obviously just wants to fuck with your head . . . which is better than fucking with your legs. Think about it, Andrew. It's cool. You're OK. Just some bored jerk in work. Probably saw you at the George or somewhere one night and . . . hates you for it. Or maybe they hate you because you get all the boys . . . oh and the cash too."

Nuala watched the red fade from Andrew's smooth cheek. He didn't have sandpaper stubble like most men. Just a plain of dark soft hair, peeping up for a breath of life before being decapitated in the morning.

Andrew opened Nuala's damaged cigarette box. He withdrew one and ran it beneath his nose. "Disgusting thing to do just for something to do," he said. "Remember Fergal McKenna?"

"Yeah – when you were a scout. He was the leader and a cop too."

"A complete fuck-wit. One day in the den he told me

that we must always remember that even when polishing the tool, our ancestors are watching from the ceiling."

Nuala laughed and said, "I don't get it."

"'Polishing the tool' is slang for masturbation."

"Masturbation?" Nuala laughed again. "I can't imagine polishing my tool."

"It just refers to boys. You have a –"

"A *flower*," said Nuala. "Well, now that I know where you are and you've grovelled for forgiveness over not cooking my dins, I shall now depart upstairs and indulge my pathetic addiction for the World Wide Wait."

"Hold on," Andrew said.

"Uh-huh."

"I need . . . I need to tell you something."

"Uh-huh." Nuala fidgeted with her cigarette box and managed to extract a creased cigarette. She glanced at the previously perfect cigarette now lying snapped between Andrew's perched elbows.

"I . . . I did something." Andrew's hands were wide and covering his face. "I did something I should never have done."

Nuala thought of the *Texas Chainsaw Massacre* and then the *Silence of the Lambs*. She couldn't remember which one featured the mask of flesh. Maybe both. Nope, she thought, couldn't be both. If it was both then it really belonged to the *Texas Chainsaw Massacre*. That came first.

"Back in Berlin . . . remember me and Liam and a few of the guys spent summer there?"

"Uh-huh. Years ago, wasn't it?"

"Nine years ago." Andrew dropped his hands and Nuala swallowed against the sight of his wide eyes. Andrew didn't look gay or straight. Andrew just looked mad. An angry type of mad.

Though there was a demented element there – controlled by two sets of interlocked fingers now resting on the table. Nuala thought he looked quite ugly and she wasn't used to that.

"Don't . . .," Nuala began before her voice dipped to a whisper, "don't lose control."

"What?" Andrew's jaw tensed as the teeth behind the skin clenched.

"Oh, you know." Nuala slid her hand across the table until it reached Andrew's clasped fingers. Her little finger raised in the air and tapped his thumb twice. Nuala felt that they should be sharing a pipe. For two people who spent so much time together they rarely ever had intimate moments. But a pipe would be too slow. That's why there are cigars. But a cigarette was even better. The world needs to consume its stimulants faster and faster. Nuala lit the creased cigarette and said, "Back in a sec."

Nuala walked into the hall and grabbed her brown leather coat. I closed Nuala's Moonage Daydream today, she thought. I answer to no one. Not even the basic rules of supply and demand.

Nuala stepped out through the glass porch and the estate didn't look expeditious or webbed in superhighways. It was raining and the concrete had turned black. The night seeped through her red fluffy slippers. Time is getting faster for everyone but me, she thought. The earth turned once – call it a day. Not any more. Now we adjust our atomic clocks for a *real* second every few years because the earth is slowing. One extra-second-a-year counts for new generations – that's strange. The earth is physically slowing – that's stranger.

There was a breeze in the air and it felt like winter.

Winter smack in the middle of summer. I've only seventy short years on this earth, she thought, and I've already wasted twenty-eight of them growing up and getting to where I am now – walking down the driveway and across the soggy fucking road like a rat listening to a flute.

The fog lights of the silver Puma glared and Nuala raised a hand to cover her eyes. The lights dipped and she hurried past the splashing din of the car's steaming bonnet.

Nuala peered inside. Shane was featureless and dark against the green dashboard glow. He was smoking and his wave was something congenial and lucid. Nuala pulled open the door and Shane squinted against the assault on his climate-controlled milieu.

"C'mon quick," he said. "You'll catch cold."

"You only get colds from touching things and breathing things – *not* by being cold, silly," Nuala said as she sat into the passenger seat. She shivered into the warmth and smoke. The cold seemed to emanate from an iced spine rather than the miserable elements. Nuala shifted her weight from one buttock to the other. "Excellent – heated seats."

"Uh-huh," Shane said and croaked something.

"What?"

Shane's eyes were narrow and his face broad with an almost inane smile. "I said, *good shit*." He waved the joint at the rear-view mirror and his eyes darted, trying to follow the reflected red streak.

"Grass?" Nuala asked.

"Hashish. Almost killed myself trying to zoom through those gates when they opened. Nearly ran someone off the road too. Can I have one of those little black boxes?"

"No and I prefer grass."

"Hashish is Arabic. Grass is too American. Too fucking strong. Hashish is Arabic."

"You said that, Shane."

"*And* source of the word 'assassin'."

Nuala accepted the squeezed joint and sucked it. It hit her throat with a pleasant strong burn. She sucked again and felt the oxygen plummet from her head, replaced by an expanse of ethereality. "You've impressed me," Nuala said and handed him back the joint.

"Cool. Is this a date?"

Nuala flipped down the sun shield and opened the make-up mirror. "If you get what you want from me, what would that 'want' be?" Nuala toyed with her fringe. She held its crooked jagged edge like a disapproving hairstylist.

Shane laughed. A slow hissing sound. He passed back the joint. "What do I want from you right now? Inside this car? Or in the grand scheme of things?"

"I suppose now, in this car." Nuala inhaled and was already facilely stoned. "Immediacy and all that."

Shane grinned. Nuala focused on his parted neat teeth and a motionless, glistening tongue. She told herself that she could do this – whatever 'this' was going to be. Her mother could do it. Andrew could do it. HornyDub could do it. "I judge by your silence that it's something rude," Nuala said and smiled at her apathetic reflection. She glanced down to her coat in case her chest was pulsating like a brown leather respirator.

"I never said anything rude." Shane stubbed out the joint and shut the ashtray.

Nuala placed her hand on his cheek. She closed her eyes and listened to her thumb make a straw-brush sweeping-sound against Shane's skin. She approved of stubble – it was like a temporary scar of life's progress. Nuala smiled. "You're just a baby."

"No. I'm an entrepreneur and I've been thinking. I . . . I should have told you this from the very beginning but I was worried that if I did say it then . . . then you would have implemented the clause from immediate effect."

"What are you talking about? Stop smoking."

"I'm saying that if you never want to see me again, you just have to say so. Like I'm not . . . I'm not a *real* stalker."

It was hot now and Nuala unbuttoned her coat. She stretched her legs. A car cruised past and bounced over the pretty tiled speed bump. It turned off the road into the house next to Andrew's. Little bodies bailed out of the car and screamed through the drizzle. She waited for Richard and Samantha, ardent Neighbourhood Watchers, to check out the mysterious silver Ford Puma. But they just went inside. No one notices the new cars.

Suddenly Nuala's hands slammed to the roof. Something had touched her leg.

"Just touching," Shane said. "Just touching. A human thing." Then he laughed. A nice sort of chuckle.

"You gave me a fright," Nuala said and swallowed.

"Boo." Shane continued laughing.

"Don't touch me unless I say so."

Shane nodded. He lit a second joint, inhaled and silently mouthed the word, "Sorry," as the thick pale smoke poured from his throat.

Nuala refocused on the make-up mirror. "Why did you put your hand on my knee?"

"I wanted to feel your leg – duh."

"I'm not being a smart-arse but why would you want to

feel my leg? I've never sat next to a man and thought, 'I must feel *this* leg'."

Shane's voice quickly lowered to an embarrassed whisper, "You know when you . . . you know . . . masturbate?"

"Uh-huh," Nuala lied.

"You might think then about feeling a man's leg?"

"Maybe."

"Well, I'm a guy and –"

"The question was hypothetical," Nuala said. She liked the intimacy of the car. Being able to hear every variation in Shane's breathing. The sudden pause and hushed grunt as he stretched a leg or reached for the joint. When he exhaled through his nose without a deep bass tone she was reminded that Shane hadn't been on this planet long enough to make an interesting mistake. "So, while I've been sitting here, talking to you, warming up from this shitty weather and feeling the texture of your stubble . . . while I was doing all this, you've been watching me and thinking about fucking me?"

Shane swallowed and leaned onto the steering wheel. "I wouldn't put it like that."

"I know you wouldn't."

"You know what your brother told me? He told me that you had a way of making short stories longish."

"Did he?" Nuala looked towards the house. "Tell me exactly what you were thinking. Like, while looking at me you were thinking of us in bed?"

Shane laughed and shook his head. "No. Jesus."

"What then?"

"Well . . . shit, you really want to know?"

"Yep."

"Right . . . if there's silence and you're watching your neighbours' car pull into the drive . . . then I might take advantage of that pause to look at your brown leather coat and think about what's beneath it. Think about feeling the tone of your flesh through your clothes. Think about squeezing your ti – breasts, weighing them in my hand. I might imagine reaching over and pulling up your dress and feeling the material of your kni – panties. Feel the heat of your pussy. I like that. I like the constant heat of the pussy. It's like an energy radiator. Is that too much information?"

Nuala looked down between the flaps of her coat to where her dress creased over her crotch. It *is* constantly warm, she thought. And now it's . . . "And when I started talking to you again, the thoughts disappear – just like that?"

"No. I touch your leg and your hands jump to the roof. Then the thoughts disappear – just like that."

Nuala thought of the boys and men and women on-line and all their strange dreams. She remembered Andrew leaving the house a hundred times, dressed to kill and wearing a saintly glow of crazy expectation. She summoned the sounds of Andrew with some new boy down below in the living-room, moving and sucking and thrusting and gasping. She thought of all the silent breakfasts, where a withered Andrew just shrugged his shoulders with blasé la-di-da at what had happened the night before. She pictured HornyDub's pretty face, full of desperate wishes. And for all those people Nuala had felt just pity and disdain. She wanted to feel it now – for Shane. But there was a throbbing between her legs.

"Can I touch you?" Shane asked.

"Where?" Nuala's shoulders involuntarily squeezed into her body.

"Between your thighs. Not beneath your dress. But over it. To feel the outline of your underwear."

"No." Nuala pouted as if the possibility had crossed her mind.

That fucking throbbing, Nuala thought. It was nice and she didn't want it to be nice. The first time she'd felt that throbbing was when she was thirteen and on a family holiday in New York. At the airport when going through security, a black guy in a uniform had frisked them all. When frisking Nuala he'd brushed against her early-breasts and inner thighs. When her parents had gone shopping in Duty Free and Andrew had made a beeline to *Burger King*, Nuala went back out to the check-in hall to queue again at the security gate.

She looked at Shane, hands on the steering wheel and watching the road as if driving through rain. She noticed the way a small vein on his temple calmly throbbed. His blood was in no great hurry – immutable – unlike this great slowing-down planet. "Da-dum, da-dum, da-dum," she said and touched the beating vein. Nuala thought about his cock. She wondered if it was erect. If she could freeze the world, she would reach over and touch it through his trousers. She would use an item instead of her hand. Her cigarette box or something.

"So what now?" Shane asked and examined himself in the rear-view mirror.

Nuala turned the glass to face her and lightly erased a tiny smudge of brown lipstick. Then she looked over to Andrew's house and saw a shadow pass the downstairs window. She turned to Shane. He'd been watching her but he quickly looked away.

"Caught ya," she said. "What were you thinking?"

"Nothing."

"Tell me." Nuala swallowed. It would be such a personal disappointment if nothing happened next.

Shane put his arms behind his head and said, "OK, I thought of you as . . . I suppose, a prostitute. No, a *whore* – better word – who does cheap neighbourhood tricks. 'Ten bucks to see my tits'. That type of thing."

"So you looked at me and thought – whore." Nuala didn't know what she wanted to happen but it *had* to be some type of baptism.

"I want you to shock me," Shane said. His lips parted with a moist smack. "You make public the private and – and by doing that you exact a divine grace on my poor weary stressed life. Look, the kids are still screaming in my head." He plugged fingers into his ears and his face crumpled in torment. "My fat dull wife is screaming inside as well. She never leaves me alone – more money, more mouths to feed. 'You are useless,' she says. 'Let's go to Mass.' All that crap . . . man, I'm wasted."

Nuala laughed. "Excellent," she said. "So you come to Dirty Nuala for shock therapy. Not relief. Relief is boring. You can get relief from your videos that you hide from the wife and kids. And despite your dreary wife you keep yourself well."

Shane nodded. "Come on, Nuala. Please. Do something. Show me."

What did Andrew say? she thought. Even when polishing the tool our ancestors are watching from the ceiling. Hi Dad.

"OK," Nuala whispered. She pulled wide the flaps of her

brown leather coat, opened her legs and glanced at Shane. He was watching, his gaze moving slowly down Andrew's white shirt, pausing at the visible black bra. His eyes continued downwards to the elastic waistband of her purple dress and further down to where blue swirls of pattern rounded the hem. Then there were her ankles – her chubby ankles that she hated. And then worse – red furry slippers.

"Go on," Shane whispered. He inhaled through his nose and swallowed. Nuala liked the terseness of his Adam's apple.

She placed a finger over his lip. "Shhh," she said. She took the hem of her dress and pulled it up. She saw her knees, firm and strong and spread. The throbbing was harder now and Shane's breathing grew more urgent but not creepy. Nuala pulled the dress up further, raising herself a few inches from the padded seat to bunch the material beneath her. She looked down. Her black panties were perfectly visible. A small string travelled around her hips centring the lace crotch-patch. Small blue ribbons decorated the panties' rim. She'd bought them over a year ago near Grafton Street in a small expensive boutique. They weren't a favourite pair.

"Amazing thighs," Shane whispered. He was staring between her strong taut legs, and Nuala felt that it was the power from his eyes that caused her throbbing.

"Can I touch myself?" he whispered without shifting his gaze.

Nuala inhaled and felt her chest rise with a power rush. "No," she said. Nuala hooked her fingers beneath the inner rim of her panties and moved them aside. There was a brief moist sound as her vaginal lips parted by their own accord. The throbbing intensified tenfold.

"Jesus," Shane whispered, "you are – you are so beautiful. I'm in pain here. I need to touch my cock."

"No," Nuala said.

"Can I smell you?" He was staring down between her legs. "Please. Just to see – just to remember. Please. *Please*."

She looked to the roof of the car. It was padded and pale. Is Shane's girlfriend watching from the roof? she thought. Is she up there with Granny and Dad?

A warm jet of air from a conditioning vent blew against her spread vagina. She looked down. It wasn't a warm jet from a conditioning vent. It was Shane's breath as he hovered inches above her right thigh.

"Your pussy hair," he whispered, "it's so long. I'm glad it's not shaved or shaped like all the others. Strands . . . strands are glued to your thigh."

"I'm going now," Nuala said.

Shane grunted and pulled himself up straight. "Give me something for later. Your panties." His expression was momentous and beads formed on his upper lip. His chest rose and fell as if he'd just run from somewhere.

"You really want my smell?"

"I'd kill for it."

She looked up to the roof again. Her eyes closed and she released the pressure. A jet of urine shot from between her spread legs to the chasm of legroom beneath the dashboard. She retracted her legs up to her seat to better control her aim. "You can smell it when I'm gone. And you can smell it tomorrow. And you can watch for months as its power rots your little-boy-racer car." Nuala stopped herself before the stream became a messy dribble. She looked to the roof. Not even her ancestors could banish the throbbing.

Nuala clicked open the passenger door. She dropped her slippered feet to the black wet concrete and dried her vagina across the passenger seat. Then she shimmied her purple dress and brown leather coat back into place.

Shane clutched the wheel as if an electric pulse gripped his fingers. "You're my fucking goddess," he said and gently rubbed his palm across the stained seat. "You're the most – the most perfect thing in the whole wide world."

"Think so?" Nuala said and closed the door. Immediately Shane fell to the passenger seat like a faulty arrow. She didn't want to see anything else. It was cold and her panties were wet. She swore she'd never wear them again.

Chapter Eight

The city was paralysed with people. Shane was waiting for the lights to change and bodies just kept pouring over the Ha'penny Bridge and under the stone archway leading to Temple Bar. He squinted across the Liffey to his apartment. Externally it looked like a row of creepy attic windows.

The lights turned green and Shane punched his horn to blow some stragglers off the street. He imagined his car letting out a flash of blinding laser rather than a crude honk. That would be impressive, he thought, but unrealistic. Everyone knows that blinding lasers are banned. What about the latest legal military technology? Order a new Puma with sky roof and an inaudible sound wave that liquefies the bowels of overconfident pedestrians; sticky foam that can superglue them to the ground; capture nets that give them cuts, chemical burns and electric shocks. But even better than all of that would be a spanking new black five-door BMW.

Shane inhaled deeply through his nose and noticed nothing. That morning when climbing into the Puma the stale urine had hit the back of his throat like odious white glue. But after a few moments his old ebullience had returned. It really was like starting out all over. Thinking about life as if it were a powerful machine pumping away in his heart made from the finest technology salvaged from the Roswell crash.

The mobile phone vibrated against his hip and Shane slipped on his driving headphones. "Yeah."

"God. I knew you wouldn't be in your office," a cacophonous voice proclaimed.

Orla! Shane thought. Orla, Orla, Orla. Right on time. Purrrr-fect-toe-ment-toe. She was at the Morrison Hotel. Sipping morning coffee with Patrick. Signing up Hieronymus Bosch for another five-year contract with her gargantuan commercial property firm. Everything suddenly falls into place. "Hi, Orla," Shane said. Then he yawned, as if the deal was the last thing on his mind. "Trust Patrick is treating you like a queen."

"Oh, Patrick – running late, I'm afraid. Just on my way there now. Don't have Patrick's number – just yours. Hence why I'm ringing. Where are you?"

"Em . . . just past the Ha'penny Bridge"

"South side?"

"Uh-huh." Shane's eyes narrowed.

"I don't believe it. Slow down. I'm at the corner of Parliament Street. Just jumped from a taxi to avoid the Quays and use the new brid – clocked you now. Shane, silver metal is such a boring boy fantasy."

Shane pulled over and thought, this isn't right. Orla opened the door and jumped in, briefcase firmly against her chest. Orla was a successful office type who prided herself on doing things out of the ordinary like parachuting for charity and then impressing her friends with how crazy she is. Orla was pregnant. It didn't suit her sharply cut brown fringe and boring shoulder-length hair. Her stomach was huge and the gradual manufacture of the child was a spectacle on her face. But she clearly loved being swollen with extra guts. She was bubbly and loud and cherished her own dismal sense of humour. It seemed a new revelation to her – the capacity to laugh loudest at her own jokes. Shane despised Orla but she was powerful and was responsible for at least sixty per cent of Shane's business.

"Shane, you're a saint," she said and slammed the door closed. Suddenly she clasped her throat as if in Darth Vader's mind-grip and rasped, "Oh my God, what is that pong?"

"Pong?" Shane said and almost lost control of the car. "Oh it's . . . it's piss."

"Jesus."

"I mean, *dog* piss."

"I *know* it's dog pee. Jesus! How can you drive with that stench? Must – open – window." Orla felt around for a non-existent handle.

Shane pressed a button. The window zoomed halfway down. "There. That better? I'm just used to it. Like cow shit in the country. You can smell it for a second. Then – abracadabra – it's gone. But it's not really gone. Your nose just doesn't register it any more."

"Yeah. Whatever. It's horrible and I can *still* smell it. Look, Shane, bad news. I'm glad we've met like this because I really didn't want to inform you of the unfortunate turn of events through Patrick. The deal's fallen through."

"The deal's what? How can it have fallen through? I haven't let it drop – have you?" Psychoneurotic pangs jutted down his arms and Shane clicked the indicator to pull into a vacant 'no parking' zone outside the huge yellow gates of Guinness's brewery. He pulled up the handbrake.

"The interior designers," Orla said while glancing at her watch, "say 'sculptures' for the docks complex. They're not anti-modern. But they *are* modern-indifferent."

Stay cool, Shane told himself. He forced himself to smile amiably and said, "But Orla, prints are much, *much* better. They don't clutter up the world so much."

Orla nodded her head with what Shane surmised to be apathy – almost as if she was unaware that this 'unfortunate turn of events' would affect his existence for the rest of his life. "It's not only that," Orla said with a shrug. "It's institutionalised vogue – change, change, change. Suits – read 'the public' – want fake Grecian statues. I suppose they just don't have much interest in high art any more."

Shane again forced himself to laugh but couldn't stop himself from saying, "That's basically because high art refuses to have any interest in the public. Cunts."

"Bingo!" Orla said.

Shit, fuck and damn, Shane thought.

"See," Orla said and beamed. "You know it too. It's like . . . do you know who's taken over an entire floor of the old Mills down at the new docks development?"

Shane shrugged. He wasn't listening. He was occupied with figuring out his net worth.

"A London multimedia publisher. They made a killing last Christmas with a *Simplify Your Life With 101 Tips* booklet."

"I hate you," Shane muttered and rubbed his forehead. A headache was building.

"Then there was the audio-tape and workbook and CD-ROM. Major credit cards accepted, of course." Orla laughed, caught her reflection in the make-up mirror and laughed harder.

"What's your point?" Shane asked and felt his smile wane.

"Doesn't it compute yet, Shane darling? Your arty-farty stuff is just *too* messy. People want to simplify their lifestyles. They want to simplify their lifestyles until they've created a lifestyle that doesn't even require their *fucking* presence." Orla's ostentatious denouncement left a big black full stop in the air. "Oh come on, Shane. Say something. You're pale."

"No, no, it's cool. Just a bit of a shock."

"Oh good. I had assumed Hieronymus Bosch could absorb this type of setback in its sleep. For a moment there, you had me worried. Thought I was putting you into an early grave or something. Oh Jesus! You know what I meant . . . *shit*."

"It's cool. Don't worry about it. You know, the world keeps spinning. Doesn't stop for me. Didn't stop for Lisa." Shane was finding it difficult to breathe. His heart was pounding and a few seconds ago it had occurred to him that he might be about to suffer a heart attack like a twenty-year-old guy he once knew who dropped dead after doing a single line of coke.

"Lisa," Orla muttered. "Met her once. Lovely girl. Such a tragedy."

Jesus Christ, Shane thought. I'm going to have to work for a living. Actually work. My car is hire purchase, I rent my TV and video, even the fucking stereo and game-console. I don't own anything. Nothing. Except for a few hundred second-hand books. Oh Jesus, no more just clocking in for the odd lunch with a cluster of suits to pass out invoices for a hundred prints. I'm going to have to *look* for business. I'm going to have to *sell* myself. "It's no problem, Orla," Shane said with a smile and cracked his knuckles. "That's business, right?"

"As you said yourself, the world doesn't stop spinning for any of us. But if anything comes up I'll be sure to think of you." Orla pulled the door handle. "I'll get out here – I've gotta be somewhere nearby." Orla had disentangled herself from Shane's car and retreated backwards until her back hit against the yellow double doors of Guinness's brewery. "Shane, I envy you. You're so young and have already come so far."

"Thanks," Shane said. "Talk to you soon, Orla. Orla?"

Orla was already cuddled into her mobile. "Not a chance . . . what? Yeah, bye Shane . . . uh-huh . . ."

Shane mounted a curb that was never *ever* supposed to be mounted. He stepped out of the car muttering, "Shit, shit, shit," and looked up at the black and glass front of the Morrison Hotel.

"Excuse me, sir," a young doorman exclaimed while pottering down the steps in silly tails and a grey cravat. "Some advice, sir. Some clever advice. You can't park there. You'll get towed. There's the sign, sir."

"Know what, Kevin?" Shane said, fingering the porter's metal nametag. "There's just one thing wrong with *you* offering people advice."

"And what's that, sir?"

"You're a porter."

Shane immediately spotted Patrick with a magazine spread before him in a darkened alcove. Despite the huge Art Nouveau bar being almost empty there was a reserved sign plonked on his table. Patrick shifted uncomfortably in his suit while talking on his mobile. "No way. I, like, totally disagree. If aliens came, they'd screw us up like we screwed up the Africans, not that I'm racist or anything. It would give us a leap forward on the evolutionary scale that we just can't deal with. We'd all end up crack addicts and wallowing victims . . . oh Shane, hi. Em . . . Orla never showed." Patrick hung up, his face etched with Shakespearean veracity.

"Talked to her," Shane said, exhaling a cloud of smoke, crossing his leg and slamming his kneecap against the underside of the metal table. "Ouch! Can we have fucking service here? Hey you!"

"Coming soon," a bored barmaid muttered.

"So's Christmas."

Patrick was alarmed. He looked left and right like a detective who couldn't catch the rabbit. "Jesus, Shane. Cool it or you'll get us barred."

"Sorry," Shane said and looked up at the barmaid. "Sorry to you too. Two vodkas, twist of lemon – make 'em big ones. One can of Red Bull. *Can*, please. *Not* a bottle."

"So, I take it you got the deal?" Patrick asked, pouring his coffee with a sigh as if he'd just commented on the weather.

"Sort of."

Patrick stopped pouring and looked up. "What do you mean 'sort off'?"

"I mean 'sort of' as in 'no'."

Shane's news didn't hit Patrick as hard as he thought it would. Patrick was more interested in staring over at some celebrity who was sitting at another table.

"You never heard of Colm Meaney?" Patrick could barely contain his indignation. "Jesus, Shane! *Deep Space* 9 . . . *The Next Generation*. He's a –" Patrick paused so he could remember how to whisper. "He's a *god*."

Patrick's lack of interest made Shane feel that he was the only one who was fucked. And in a way he was. If Hieronymus Bosch went to the wall then he'd walk into another arty position somewhere else. He'd always done better than Shane at college. And everyone liked him.

It suddenly occurred to Shane that he didn't even have a pension plan. I'm going to be poor, he thought. I could end up with nothing. Really nothing. Like a council house person or something. Orla – bitch, bitch, *fucking* bitch.

Shane closed over his face with his hands and inhaled. He didn't know whether it was his imagination or not, but he caught Nuala's raw scent from his fingers. Shane downed his second drink and ordered another two large ones and a fresh pot of coffee for Patrick. Nuala, he thought, and beneath the table gave his cock a gentle-teasing squeeze.

Patrick was talking. "So last night, when you didn't show, I went straight to the RDS."

"The Car Show?" Shane leaned back into his chair and laughed.

"I *had* to see the Bond car. Anyway, met a girl. A librarian."

Shane was still laughing.

"Turns out she knows Hieronymus Bosch and had bought a print from you. So while we're talking – and get this – she looks into my eyes and asks, like she's asking about a William Blake or something, she asks . . ." Patrick paused to observe Shane staring at his empty glass and turning it round and round as if screwing it into the black metal table. He cleared his voice and continued. "OK Shane, we'll talk about you. Yeah, Nuala seems dead on. Know what you should do, bud? You should release a press statement . . . something to the effect that reports of your death have been greatly exaggerated. You know, that Paul McCartney, Abbey Road thing."

"Mark Twain," Shane said and sighed. "It's Mark fucking Twain. I hope that sometime in the future I'll be really embarrassed about this day. Most memories already embarrass me. I suppose that's because the person I share them with is dead. You can't . . . correct them. You can't justify yourself. When Lisa and me first got together, I remember I had great plans. Huge plans. We sat in a boat down the country, absolutely hammered . . . and I told her that I was certain I was going to be huge. Like famous. Massively successful. I was sure something would come along besides our print shop . . . movies, directing, who knows? And she believed me and she told me then that she loved me. That was the first time. 'I love you, Shane, because you're not like anyone else. You'll be able to do anything.'" Shane pressed the back of his head against the hard rim of the metal chair. "I was so full of shit," he said. "I was her life and I let her down over and over again."

"Jesus . . ." was all Patrick could manage.

Shane sat back and loosened his shoulders against the methamphetaminic rush of two double vodkas and Red Bull. He needed that. He didn't like being afraid and his future was now dark and uncharted. If it wasn't for Nuala, he thought, the only thing I'd have to do with my life would be to work for a living. And that's a paradox. But Nuala is something good. That's all I'm sure of. I don't even know what I really think of her. "I don't even know what I really think of Nuala," Shane mused aloud. "We're still at that stage of getting to know each other. At least I think it's a stage. It's weird. She's older then me. I never went out with someone who's older than me. But maybe that's it – this is Nuala, can she be of assistance to you? And if that's all there is to her then –"

"So it's . . . not love then?" Patrick asked, while having another three-second stare at Colm Meaney.

"Didn't say that. I don't fucking know, Patrick. You're asking awkward questions, you know?" Shane leaned across the table until only inches separated their faces.

Patrick swallowed and blinked. He loosened his necktie and scraped his chair out a few inches from the table. "I think," Patrick whispered, "I think Nuala is . . . really cool. Really nice. But be careful in case you're on a sort of – of *rebound* trip." He quickly licked his lips as if mopping up scarce pride.

Shane upturned his empty glass and dropped two melting ice cubes into his palm. "How can you say that to me, you fuck?" He shook his fist as if he was about to roll dice. "Come on, what nasty button did I press in your head? I want to know. Tell me, how can you say that to me? I'm supposed to be your fucking mate!"

"Jesus, Shane –"

Shane flung the ice cubes. Patrick raised an arm too late and they smacked against his cheek and forehead.

"Ow! Come on, Shane! Take it easy. I'm sorry. You're causing a scene."

"A scene," Shane muttered. He stood up and back-heeled his chair across the bar. "This," he shouted, "is a fucking scene!"

"I'm sorry, bud. Sorry." Patrick was pale and gritting his teeth against his trembling frame. He looked left and right and made a thumbs-up gesture to the bar staff in the background. "Really, Shane. I didn't mean anything by it. I swear. I mean I would never –"

"I have to go," Shane calmly announced while repeatedly rubbing the tip of his nose. "See ya."

* * *

Around the corner from Rennes, Saunière & Château a small queue was building outside the Bailey. Andrew skipped it, nodded to the doorman and the doorman said, "Andy," and smiled as if he'd just uttered some valuable password. The Bailey was a bar that had recently butchered all its character and buried the cadaver beneath designer neon wall murals, fifteen-seater tables and a nightclub sound system. The bar staff dressed like eighties Wall Street brokers and the waitresses were all French and Spanish students. Andrew hated the place.

Andrew walked across the bar to his work crowd's usual table beneath a glowing green neon sign that advertised nothing but a Japanese alphabetical symbol. A murmur spread around the table like happy dominoes.

Matt stood up. "Hey Andy, didn't think you were coming." In the background beneath the music and the shouting and Matt's panting breath, someone tutted.

"Are you writing those letters?" Andrew asked. He faced Matt with a thunderbolt poise that said he'd prefer to lose than be timid.

"What? Ha! We're staying here before heading onto Lillies later." Matt gulped down his whiskey and wiped the sweat from his brow. He swung his golden key ring that was also a member's tag. "Barry and Roy are bringing those two little ladies. Jesus, I can't remember their names. So you're coming, yeah?"

"Did you write those letters?"

"Ah man, can those can'ts. It's cosy in the Library."

Andrew grabbed Matt by his tie knot and pulled his sweating face up to his own. "Listen . . . I *know* it's you."

"What *the* fuck, Andy?" Matt swallowed and wore an expression of resigned incomprehension.

"The letters," Andrew spoke calmly into his face.

"What fucking letters? Jesus . . ."

Andrew released him. "Nothing, Matt. Nothing."

"Don't give me that. What fucking letters?"

Andrew pushed his way back through the crowd. Outside his black BMW was getting clamped.

* * *

Shane hated graveyards. They sucked his energy. He'd gone once on a bank holiday and was amazed at how packed the place was with the living. Lisa's graveyard was the nicest one in Dublin. Shane was convinced of this even though he hadn't been to all the others. It was so pretty and graveyards were not supposed to be pretty. There were finely groomed tall hedges to shroud it from the road and curling flower-lined pathways that encouraged a stroller to stroll forever. The tour de force was at the back of the graveyard where the gravestones ceased at a low wall. On the other side was a fifty-foot drop down a red-stone cliff to the sea. And the sea stretched to the distance. And in the distance was invisible England. Lisa's grave had a view of the sea.

The headstone was new. Lisa's family had never called to tell Shane it had been put in site. They'd never approved of Shane in the first place.

Shane lifted a foot and like a cautious horse utilised his heel to test the sturdiness of the flat marble plaque. There was just her name, date of birth and death and a biblical quotation so lame that if Lisa had been a soothsayer, she would have made Shane swear never to allow it chiselled above her details.

Shane breathed deeply. The sea always stirred the wind and even on hot summer days there was a chill. It was worse today – the sky was overcast and Shane saw his future somewhere up there in God's exhaled smoke.

When standing over the grave Shane was always aware that Lisa was just five feet away. He once woke in the middle of the night in a blind panic before frantically rooting out photographs because he just couldn't remember her face.

When the body had been returned to Dublin, he'd sat in the morgue, gazing down on her perfect ashen countenance as if he was a physiognomist. He'd tried to picture the funeral house where the embalming technique would mechanically suck the juices out of the corpse and replace them with preservatives. His dead girlfriend wouldn't be allowed to sit up, fart, and twitch, like the dead ones of the past. Embalming would ensure that everyone who would see Lisa in the next two days would be under the illusion that death is nothing but another stage of her life.

Shane pushed down with his shoe on the marble slab and then lifted his foot. He left behind a sandy footprint. Lisa's chiselled name would stay but his stamp would be taken by the wind.

"What's happening, Lisa?" Shane whispered. "I feel like I've sold my soul." They'd known each other when growing up in a posh suburb. But then they lost contact until the opening night of Hieronymus Bosch. She'd been marching through the empty mall, singing in chorus with a gang on a hen night. He'd told them to shut up and she'd told him to fuck off. Two weeks later they were living together in his apartment and every day was new. If he'd ever asked a trivial question Lisa would drag him around the library until she'd found the correct book and then she'd look up the relevant chapter while he'd mutter in the background about the books being just for decoration. And when Lisa died it had felt like all the libraries in the world had suddenly burnt up.

"I don't see my parents any more," he whispered. "I know you'd want me to but I don't." He closed his eyes and like some comic book superhero imagined his mind beaming through the slab of marble to some world where Lisa was alive and listening and omniscient.

It made sense to Shane, not to see his parents any more. One of the reasons people move house is not to live among old regrets. Shane had exorcised the aura of grief from his apartment and flung those demons into his childhood house. Now he hated that place. It still had a rotatory phone – when it rings, it *rings*. Even outside of the house Shane didn't like meeting his parents. It was their eyes. Meeting Neil Armstrong, all over again.

"I should be missing you till death," Shane muttered. Instead he was waking in the night, with Nuala on his mind while his semen spilled like boiling acid all over his bedclothes.

Shane surveyed the entire graveyard and the sea and took it all in as if he was leaving a perfect holiday resort for home. There was hardly anyone around. Just the odd moth-eaten widow or grandparent and grandchild disappearing behind old erect gravestones before reappearing on a pathway to a car. He looked at the sea and focused on the waves. They seemed to be moving eastwards. "See ya, Lisa."

* * *

Nuala was nearing the end of a typical day. She sat on a stool behind the counter of Nuala's Moonage Daydream sighing at her watch as it approached the time when she would have to tediously tot up the day's minuscule takings and compare them to her till roll. Of course there was always more money *in* the till than on the roll.

She looked at her half-smoked cigarette. Smoking had become the most complicated thing to do in the world. It made her think about death twenty times a day. It also reminded her of Andrew twenty times a day. She stared into the red of the cigarette. Andrew had always nagged her with the theory that all smokers must hate themselves since each pull is really a self-inflicted wound on their lungs. Nuala stabbed it out and thought, I don't hate myself.

"Time crawls," she muttered and *ka-chinged* the cash register. Last week she'd seen a rerun of the first episode of *Lost in Space* in all its black and white glory. It was set far in the future. 1997 to be exact. Nuala had come to the conclusion that boredom is the most boring of words. She much preferred the 'languishment of inattention' but didn't know if 'languishment' was a real word or not. Nuala wanted to open the drawer beneath her right elbow. Her daily tarot reading was spread out inside the desk. The Moon was never a good card. But an inverted Moon was the worst.

"Something is going to be awful."

Chapter Nine

Shane stirred his coffee. He couldn't get enough of Nuala. Last night he'd talked to her on the phone for an hour. He'd wanted to tell her about his problems but she'd done all the talking. He could listen to her for an entire week. Now it was a new day and Nuala had brought him out on an afternoon date.

"So you're Shane," Nuala's mother said. "And you're in . . . you do what?"

"Mam," Nuala said and threw her eyes to the ceiling. "He's an art-guy. Not an *arty*-guy. Hence the silver hairdresser's-Porsche you spied on through the corner of your front blinds. You *are* aware that you're not invisible? Like, that by shifting the curtain an inch the whole curtain moves?"

"On and on she goes," Nuala's mother said with a smile and a sigh. "And when she stops nobody knows."

Shane laughed and stirred his coffee. The radio was on in the background. There was a public transport strike in the city, a global computer company was going bust because its new billion-dollar software is suddenly old and a tourist was stabbed on Grafton Street.

"Why are you ironing?" Nuala asked while rooting through the cupboards.

"I forgot it was Joan's week off."

"Joan?" Shane said, deciding he'd better say something.

"Cleaning lady," Nuala said with a minor deep echo from speaking into a compact cupboard.

"Christ, I'm never doing this again." Nuala's mother said while flattening a tee shirt with metal heat. "People who do this – iron their underwear every week – they mustn't like living."

Nuala perched her elbows on the tip of the ironing board and announced, "I despise the cleaning lady."

"Don't be horrible," her mother said.

"Sorry."

"Horrible girl," Nuala's mother mumbled while the iron spat some steam.

"Mam, you're like a squirrel or something. Storing, storing, storing. Crap, junk . . . syrup? Why syrup? You'd kill yourself before you'd eat something as fattening as syrup. Just because someone brings it back as a gift from Canada doesn't mean you have to keep it forever."

Nuala's mother rested the iron upright. "Squirrel, she says. So what? I can't think of one single animal that's well known for throwing things out."

"Very clever, Mam," Nuala said and smirked at Shane. "Only one, two, *three* more of my blouses to go before *all* my socks."

"I can't believe you still do your daughter's washing," Shane said.

"Well, Shane, in time you'll learn that Nuala is truly useless at anything useful. How she hasn't run that shop into the ground is beyond me. 'Potions and lotions made to go'?" She put down her iron to laugh in an amazed way. "I just don't know. I just don't know at all."

Shane laughed while watching Nuala. She'd withdrawn her head from the cupboard and her big forehead was blanketed in a frown. "Right, Shane," she said. "Time to make yourself useful. Get to work."

Shane took a deep drag of his cigarette and stabbed it out. He stood up and nodded a smile to Nuala's mother. He walked through the broad hall and out through the double front doors to the gravel of a driveway spacious enough for four cars. The boot of his silver Puma opened with a smoker's gasp. He hooked his fingers beneath the first of three large black plastic sacks. He had no idea what was in them but his mission was to shift them from the car to the hallway. They felt like floppy bodies.

He remembered gazing down on Lisa's open coffin and soaking up harmony. Yet he had known that death was not quiescent. Lisa had been eating herself from within in a final burst of appetite. The digestive juices had already turned on the very organs that had held them stable for over two decades. The bacteria that had always been a part of her were suddenly partaking in a feast like they'd never known before. Lisa's meat was now fuel for a billion strange forms of microscopic life.

Shane saw himself back in his Lanzarote hotel room waiting for Lisa's return. Lisa was a slob and he couldn't settle until bringing some form of utilitarianism back to the room. He'd scooped her second- and third-choice outfits from the white tiled floor and flung them into her case. His stomach was a dead weight. Something was in it but was definitely anaesthetised and not moving for the foreseeable future.

It was hot. The air-conditioning was antiquated so Shane shuffled out of his clothes, grabbed a joint, turned off the lights and stepped onto the balcony. It was nice being naked in the night air. With the palm trees on the beach swishing, with a nail-clipped moon and the submarine lights of the pool – he could pretend that he was somewhere decent. Feeling pleasantly stoned Shane closed his eyes, snapped them open and stared at the night. "Jesus," he said, "what have I done?"

His watch said midnight. He'd left her an hour ago. How could he have left his girlfriend with Soeren Halkier? He pictured Soeren's face. Nothing twisted in there. He was just a guy on holidays with his recently divorced father. Shane didn't know where Soeren was staying. All he knew was that he drove a rented black jeep.

Shane went inside and made coffee. This time a cigarette tasted nice. It's paranoia, he thought, that's all. How many single women were out cruising Avenida de la Playa tonight? Hundreds. Nothing would happen to Lisa. He was being stupid. He settled into the sofa, grabbed a pen and paper and began to scribble.

> *Cancer, heart attack, stroke,*
> *haemorrhage, suffocation, infection,*
> *despair.*

They were all the natural causes of death that he could think of. He tagged on *Soeren Halkier* and laughed. "Prick."

He squatted to the floor with his back against the door. Feeling wide-awake and bored, he had time to wait. Ten minutes passed as he listened to the hotel's night-time noise. Hollow echoes from down the marble staircase and the futurist hum of the imperceptible air-conditioning. He thought of Lisa's thong and her naked legs and short black mini and her perfectly contoured back. He thought of Soeren.

Finally he heard footsteps. Someone was climbing the hotel's cold marble stairs. Click-click. A woman. It had to be Lisa. He smelled his armpits and waited.

With the car boot now empty, Shane slammed it shut.

"Good boy," Nuala said as she stepped out through the porch. "Come on, I want to show you something."

The small wooden door to the side passageway was open and Nuala breathlessly disappeared down it. Shane followed. The house was deep. Frosted window after frosted window ran by his peripheral vision and then his shoes smacked across the pink-tiled veranda. The garden was so neat and sculptured it seemed as if a computer had designed it. Rose bushes and hanging vines. Hedges shaped into rotund pillars, a glasshouse with tables of shrubs, and stepping-stones mapping pathways across the recently cut grass. Even the bees bouncing around the gaping blooms seemed tamed. And at the end of the garden was a small artificial pond. Nuala was already sitting cross-legged on its neat grassy shore. "C'mon, sit," she ordered.

"OK." Shane sat opposite and also crossed his legs.

"Postural echo," Nuala said and smirked. "You know, Shane, Dublin's all right. But when sitting here and remembering camping out in the same spot with Andrew when we were kids . . . we had a wigwam. And it was just like the countryside. Now in Hill View Estate I miss the stars. Our garden is too small there. Always full of light. Me and Andrew would lie here at night staring up at the stars and trying to fathom how many there were. Ever since then the sky has been sort of disappointing. At night when you look in the pond you can see the reflection of the stars. The last time I did that I was able to count the stars around my feet. And when I flicked away my fag some of the stars disappeared in a ripple."

"There's – there's fish in the pond," Shane said as he squinted into the murky green. "Fucking big ones too."

"A cousin of ours pissed me off when I was fourteen. He was staying for the weekend and was a little shit. Kept knocking on my bedroom door and running off. So one night I brought him down here to the pond and sat him down just where you are and tearfully explained that although he believed he was ten, he was in fact fifteen and mentally retarded. I told him that it was only fair he knew, as his parents and his 'friends' would never tell him as long as they thought he was happy. Later, Andrew killed me. He always killed me over things like that. God, it's a nice day." Nuala uncrossed her legs and stretched herself against the grass. Her right hand dipped its fingers into the pond.

Shane was glad she'd shut her eyes. She was so beautiful he just wanted to stare down on her. I love you, he thought. Then he took a deep breath and said, "Having a pond and garden like this – it would make me want to get out of the city every weekend."

Behind her closed eyes Nuala lazily smiled. "Last year after a bad week in work – the type of week that makes you realise that life is one crap hour after another crap hour and so what if one day there's only nanoseconds left. So on the Friday I rang the airport and got them to list that night's flights with available seats. I went home to Andrew – told him I would be staying the night here in Mam's and taxied on out to the airport. Five hours later I was leaning over the Ponte Vecchio in Florence, looking down on the rushing Arno river, staring up at the Duomo and thinking to myself . . . actually I don't know what I was thinking to myself. I went clubbing that night – sort of. There aren't any clubs in Florence. None. Just café bars that play music. I sat in one till five AM and then bussed it to the airport. I was back home by midday. And no one knows I did that."

"Wow," Shane said. "That's cool."

"Shane?" Nuala again stretched herself against the grass. A goldfish came up to nibble one of her lazy fingers and she giggled at the sensation. "What do men see in an asshole?"

"I don't see anything in an asshole," Shane said. His eyes closed. It was nice talking to Nuala's voice. It was like a rolling conversation in a most comfortable deep dream. "I stay away from them. The last time I came across an asshole was at Lisa's funeral. A guy I went to school with – Ross. I was told later that Ross uses the obituary column to look up old schoolmates. You know? When their parents die or something? Then he's there – puff – just like that. Still trying to make friends after all these years. What an asshole, huh?" Shane listened to Nuala laugh quietly. Then she sighed.

"I don't mean people, ninny. I mean . . . I mean . . . a few weeks ago I was on the toilet. The door to the bathroom was half-open and Andrew was walking by on the landing. And I asked him, what do you find attractive about the asshole?

I'll always remember how he looked at me. It was a look of disgust. He didn't say anything but just closed over the bathroom door. That was the last time I casually took a pee without closing the door. We used to have great conversations with me on the toilet and him coming and going as he watered his plants on the landing window. But never again. Not after that."

Shane didn't feel relaxed any more. He didn't like talking about assholes. At the top of the garden he saw Nuala's mother. "Here comes your mum."

Nuala sat up and yawned at the sun. "Do you know what the best thing is about this pond? It makes you think about things like throwing the latest NASA computer and a dog into the pond and then waiting to see which one climbs out first. See Shane, technological advances have replaced evolution. And evolution was never any good. It never made us better. It just made us different . . . I want my fucking tail back."

Shane didn't know whether to laugh or nod his head as if she'd said something important. So instead he lit up a cigarette.

"Hi, Mam," Nuala shouted when her mother reached the halfway point between house and pond. Then she lowered her voice and said, "I think of Mam's funeral a lot. That will be the test. And I don't know whether caring will mean passing or failing that test."

Her mother sauntered across the lawn with big black sunshades resting above her forehead. She was carrying a tray with two cups of coffee.

Nuala took Shane's cigarette and inhaled. "Shane was very helpful bringing in all that stuff. He's earned one of Mam's cookies. Hasn't he, Mam?"

"Yes, Nuala," her mother said with a customary sigh and a shake of her head. She turned to Shane and said, "You're very good to help Nuala with –"

"Mam!" Nuala snapped.

"Opps," her mother said and tittered.

"Well . . . it was no problem." Shane swallowed. He found it hard to talk.

"And how did you and Nuala meet?"

Nuala took the tray and walked over to the garden table. She poured a lot of milk into one cup. Then she paused and lingered over it. She splashed in some more.

"How did we meet," Shane said, thinking aloud. "She . . . was buying some prints. Art prints and –"

"But what about Barbados? Nuala said you first met there." She fixed her blonde hair with a clip and snapped the finger of a red rubber gardening glove. "That girl – she never tells me anything in order. A fuddled mind she has. She's a *very* strange girl."

"Jesus!" Nuala shouted, spun around and slapped her fist into her opened palm. "I can never get my coffee right. Never!"

"A very strange girl," her mother repeated.

As Shane watched Nuala spill her coffee over a rose bush, he muttered, "She's a fucking nutcase, all right."

"Well, I haven't heard it put like that before."

"Oh, I didn't mean . . ."

But Nuala's mother had already walked away.

* * *

Tone'n'Health Club had three small compact steam rooms and three golden heated saunas. Andrew sat in one of the steam rooms. It reminded him of an overlooked 70's sci-fi film: the white plastic arced-bench beneath lights that blended into the dense suffocating steam and white ceiling. Andrew loved the steam capsules. All white, like a hot freezer. It froze time. A white towel was wrapped around his waist. He was thinking of his sister and how she'd disappeared when he'd tried to tell her his secret. Everyone loves secrets but Nuala walks out doors to avoid them. Perhaps he had overstepped some invisible mark. Perhaps they weren't as close as he'd assumed.

Andrew examined his chest. Around the nipples was an uneven spread of golden hairs deepening to black. They seemed out of place in the steam room. He loosened the towel and examined his midriff. Not bad, he thought. When all was said and done he looked in great shape.

The door creaked. Andrew stared up: hoping his withered glare would encourage the trespasser to choose one of the other free rooms. It didn't.

"Ah Andy, all alone?" The man was about fifty with a diminutive white towel held in place by the weight of a stomach fold crashing over his waist. He sat at the far end of the arced-bench and nodded. "Poor old Eddie. What a life, huh? Loyal though. Getting hospitalised for you."

Andrew's mind was blank. Then something fluttered into it. Berlin, Berlin, Berlin. Andrew scratched his face. "Tom, did you say '*for me*'?"

"Em, yeah. No one tell you? Oh dear." Tom slid down the bench and spread his arms further until the fingers of his left hand were almost touching Andrew's shoulder. His feet stretched forward and his fat pale hairy legs parted. "It was me who found him . . . crawling – *literally* crawling – on the floor in the toilet across the road. He was in a bad way. God, his jaw. Says some garda – well he didn't use the term garda – but he said, some garda had done him over."

"What's that got to do with me?" Andrew's jaw clenched.

"Well, according to Eddie – now I could hardly make this out – God, his jaw . . . but apparently the garda in question was inquiring about you. He must have recognised you or something. You were poor Eddie's last customer."

"I was?" The words sounded as if they'd squeezed out between his eyelids rather than his mouth. Andrew covered his face with his hands and breathed deeply. Stay calm, he told himself. Stay calm.

"Poor Eddie. I know he was rough but if he cleaned himself up he could pass for half the guys on my son's rugby team. I can't believe the police would do that. It's not poor Eddie's fault. I mean there's so much sex available that it demands that men – even *family* men – must focus on their sexual needs."

Andrew retracted his arms and stood up. "Don't know what's wrong with me," Andrew muttered while tightening the towel around his waist. "I just can't clear my mind."

Tom looked up at him with his yellowish eyes and said, "Too many things on it?"

Andrew remembered something somebody had said to him recently. He couldn't remember whom. "Tom, when all is said and done nothing is complicated. That's why I'm going to go home now and watch a porn or something." But the idea of porn turned sour even before Andrew had reached the locker room. He remembered the new relevance pornography had taken now that most of the performers in his collection were suddenly, overnight, younger than he was. I'm turning into Tom, he thought. I'm turning into a dirty old man.

Shane was spread on the floor at the foot of his couch. It was an effort to breathe. His chest would not expand enough to ingest all the oxygen needed. The belt buckle of his black jeans was undone and the zipper lowered. His black shirt was unbuttoned to his flat stomach. He turned his head and felt the cool varnished floorboards freeze his cheek. Nuala was sitting on a high-back leather chair. He focused on her feet. They were big feet with spread toes. The nails were painted a deep purple. Such perfection. And Nuala didn't even wear sandals.

"*Medicine*," Nuala muttered. "*New Age Cures*, *The Spices of Life*, *Aloe Vera*, *Ancient Gnostic Healing*, *North American Indian Remedies for* – Jesus, if you want old ideas read a new book."

Shane's eyes followed her feet to her ankles and then up to those beautiful calves and knees and spread thighs. She'd already caught her breath again. Her white Levis were heaped on the floor beside the leather chair. Nuala still wore her white tee shirt but it was bunched up beneath her chin. Her heavy breasts were firm and brown and somehow even better then he'd imagined they would be.

Nuala stood up, pulled off her tee shirt and ran a finger along the hardback titles. Shane watched her weight shift from one leg to the other. As she did so, each buttock tensed like the fibre bundles of a muscleman's biceps.

"Shane," Nuala said, "you're such a spa. I would have thought you were above falling for millennium fetishism.

The End of Affluence, *The End of Desire*, *The End of Economic Man*, *The End of Fame*, *The End of History*, *The End of Ideology*. Jesus – and they aren't even a series."

"It's just that they're all the same size," Shane muttered and squinted at her ass and noticed how the crack blended into the thoroughfare of her arched central spine. Her back rivalled Lisa's. He thought of the twenty or thirty '*Death of*' titles that littered his library. *Death of the Alphabet*, *Innocence*, *Magic*, *Art*, *Certainty*, *Patriarchy*, *Days*, *Sanity* and *Sorrow*. There were others.

Nuala moved further along the main library wall. "These books over here are better," she said. She was standing at an angle to him. The pale glow from a lampshade accentuated her swath of pubic hair. Shane could count individual strands. One, two, twenty-five. So fucking perfect, he thought. From this angle her belly-button ring looked like a metal hoop. He felt like stretching and stretching until his finger hooked through it and pulled her in. Then he would somehow find the strength to make love to her. They'd done everything but that. And doing everything but that had sapped him dry.

"*Streamlining Your Life*, *How to Have a 48-Hour Day*," Nuala continued with a finger poised before her lips. "I like these books. I might borrow some. *The Organising Guide for Busy Couples*. Hmmm."

That was one Lisa had bought for him and not just because it fitted. Shane had liked getting presents. Solid proof that he had been on her mind. Nuala rocked back and forth and Shane wondered how the cool wooden floor didn't numb her feet like it had frozen his cheek. "Nuala, know what the saddest fact in the world is?"

"Uh-huh." Nuala didn't turn around.

"Lisa thought she did."

"Lisa?" Nuala looked over her shoulder.

"It was a something I told her. We were skiing in Austria. And the lift-thing had broken, leaving us wobbling in that cable chair about fifty feet above a small frozen lake at the bottom of the mountain. So we're rocking there, trying to keep warm and it's snowing. Lisa says something like, 'Snow is so peaceful, the most peaceful thing in the world. It doesn't even disturb the lake when it hits it. The snow just vanishes'."

"Thought it was a frozen lake?" Nuala asked and turned back to the library wall.

"Most of it was frozen but the bit beneath us was close to a waterfall which kept the water still or normal or liquid – OK? Anyway, I told her that a silent snowflake screams when it hits the water and –"

"Screams?" Nuala stared down on Shane.

"Yeah – screams. Supersonically or subsonically or whatever. Saw it one night on the *Discovery Channel.* We need listening equipment to hear it. But fish don't. When snow is falling and children are playing and sleigh-bells are ring'n', freaked-out fish are diving to the depths of the rivers and lakes, aborting their eggs and becoming mentally deranged."

"Well done, Shane. You proved that nothing in this world is peace. Not even a fucking snowflake. You miss her?"

"Sometimes." Shane remembered watching *Miss World* with Lisa and grading the backs of the contestants. Not one of them measured up to Lisa's *ten.* But Nuala's back . . . Nuala's back draws equal.

Nuala crossed the floor until her toes touched Shane's elbow. Her toes were warm. "You think I'm better than Lisa?" She stood astride him and lowered herself onto his stomach. Shane inhaled and tensed, expecting her weight to starve his stomach of oxygen. But Nuala supported her weight within a squat. She was holding *The Organising Guide for Busy Couples*.

"That's a horrible question." Shane said and swallowed nervously.

"Bullshit," Nuala said and dangled the big hardback by a single page over his head. There was a ripping sound. "Come on. Tell me. I know you want *me* more."

Shane watched the book rock precariously above his head.

"Misery guts," Nuala stated and dropped the book. Just in time Shane shifted his head and the hardback smacked to the wooden floor with a thud. A sweep of Nuala's hand brushed it under the couch. "I think your card is The Seven of Cups. You should count your blessings. You're young, rich but not happy and that's so much better than being young, poor and not happy."

"Business is crap." Shane closed his eyes and swallowed. The future was suddenly everywhere. "I got bad news recently. I'm . . . I'm twenty-three and I suppose I'm bankrupt." He laughed and wondered why laughing didn't make it feel better. "Even when I hear myself say that, I still can't believe it. I'm broke . . . imagine that. Shane – broke."

"I still think you should count your blessings."

"Count my bless – oh!" Shane was winded. Nuala had released her weight onto his stomach. Her arms fell forward and pinned his wrists above his head.

"Is that all there is to you?" Nuala whispered into his ear. "Like . . . that's it? Your girlfriend dies and it's tragic but a small tragedy in the grand scheme of things. If it was so bad, you'd be dead now. Wouldn't you? You weren't that close to her. You're too young. And now there's business problems. So . . . *I mean*, so fucking what? I think you're a victim. I think you enjoy the lifestyle of a victim. Either that or there's something else. Well, Shane-the-victim, is there something else? Is Shane-the-victim a pseudonym for someone much more interesting?"

"I – can't – fucking – breathe."

"Sorry." Nuala let her knees take some of her weight but her hands still pinned his wrists to the floor. Her face leaned into his and she sniffed. "In my job, scent is everything. Women pick their creams and face masks and all that kind of stuff – not for what it can do to them – but from how it smells. Most of my stuff I order over the Internet and plonk it into jars and tubs labelled *Nuala's Moonage Daydream*. But the best stuff, I make myself. Out in the backroom of Nuala's empire. And the best of the best I keep *just* for myself. You only look young when you look younger than everyone else your own age. And if my little venture has taught me just one thing then it's how to smell things properly. You see, Shane-the-victim, odours are like spirits. They really are. They can be tender. Sometimes they're angry and smelly. Other times they're full of shock. And I don't smell a victim off you. I smell something else entirely."

"I'll tell you my secret, Nuala, if you want." Shane forced his arms together and Nuala's face elevated up from his head.

"Oh good, so you're not Shane-the-victim. There *is* something else."

"Uh-huh."

Nuala outstretched her arms and with a masculine grunt rose from the squatting position. She walked over to the marble fireplace and the diamond-shaped mirror. Looking into it, she fixed her crooked fringe. Then she turned and said, "OK, Shane, shoot."

Shane soaked her in. Naked. Arms folded. One leg raised onto the marble of the fireplace, the other leg slightly bent at the knee. Her bush of pubic hair was a black hole in the dim orange light and her pierced belly-button was an abstract glimmer. The most perfect creature in the whole world was now sexless.

Shane sat up and rested his back against the couch. He rotated his shoulders to loosen his muscles. After lighting a cigarette and draining Nuala's wine glass, he quickly recited the story about Lisa's last hours in Lanzarote. He breezed through it until he came to Soeren Halkier.

"What was he like?" Nuala asked, lighting her own cigarette.

"Like nobody. Like nobody we know," Shane said and continued in a drone. "Met him for a drink and I went home early. Lisa followed an hour later and –"

"Why did you go home early?"

"Cramps. Sensitive stomach."

"Poor baby. Go on."

Shane remembered waiting for Lisa to return. The noise of her footsteps on the corridor, the shake of the key against the lock. She came into the hotel room looking pale and stunned. Her eyes were squinting as if she couldn't see properly. "When she got back . . . she wasn't even late. I asked her how it went and for a second of clarity she ran through her evening with Soeren in a nothing-much-to-report kind of way. But then it all tailed off in a mumble. And then she froze."

"She froze?" Nuala's head shot forward.

"Yeah, she froze. Standing at the end of the bed. She'd just been mumbling something about not being able to hear Soeren speak because of the salsa band with funny Mexican hats." Shane remembered how she'd staggered backwards. "So I'm standing at the end of the bed and I say, 'What's up?' or something and she's just going red and swallowing a lot. Darting eyes . . . all that shit. But I insisted, sort of calmly, 'Tell me, tell me, tell me,' but she just kept freaking out. I grabbed her – by the top of her tee shirt, put my forehead against hers and said, 'Calm fucking down.'"

Shane lit another cigarette even though the first one still smoked in the ashtray. He remembered every inch of Lisa's expression. When he thought of her now, she always wore that face. A face of wide resignation. "See, I was stoned on grass and getting paranoid and I thought Lisa had taken something with Soeren and it all made sense, you see."

"And had she taken anything?" Nuala asked.

Shane closed his eyes. He wished he could close his ears. He could hear Lisa say, 'Oh God, Shane . . . Oh God . . . what's happening to me?'

"What did she say?" Nuala asked.

"She said nothing," Shane replied and swallowed. "She just backed away and stumbled on one of her shoes lying on the ground. She was always such a slob. She stumbled and fell backwards. Straight over like a fucking tree. She fell beside the wall separating the bedroom from the bathroom. And when I bent down to her – she was dead."

"Jesus," Nuala muttered. She exhaled her cigarette like she was a naked suit at an exclusive business club.

"I knew she was dead. Her head . . . it flopped forward when I raised it. Her body flat on the floor."

"What had she taken?"

"Nothing. They didn't even need to investigate the whole thing. The autopsy immediately knew what it was. It was my fault really."

"Jesus, Shane, what actually happened?"

"All week . . . I'd told her to wear her thongs. I like thongs. But she was having her period and said she couldn't. And I begged her . . . you know, we're on holidays and all that. So she went downstairs to the hotel shop and bought tampons. She never wore them . . . always one of those pad-nappy things. She died of toxic shock. It had been killing her all week. The symptoms were there. Fever at night, fucked-up stomach, weakness . . . Jesus, even a fucking rash on her back. But I thought . . . I thought it was a bug. Just a fucking bug. A chance in a million, I suppose. And the worse thing is, it fucking embarrasses me. You know . . . people asking, 'What happened to Lisa? Poor Lisa. How did she die?' And I can't say . . . I just *can't* fucking say that she died of toxic shock from a tampon."

"Was Lisa . . . was she sexy? Like did she want it all the time?" Nuala's eyes squinted as she searched for the right words.

"Jesus – I just told you that in some ways I killed my girlfriend."

"And I just asked you was she . . . hot?"

Shane stood up without a grunt. He felt elasticated with a strange adrenaline. "Haven't you heard a thing I've said?"

"Was she the best – the best in bed you've ever had? Tell me something . . . tell me a filthy fact about her."

"No – I'm not telling you anything. For fuck sake, Nuala, she's dead."

Nuala was getting annoyed. "I'm serious."

"So am I."

Ding-dong-ding. The doorbell sounded. Shane watched Nuala and Nuala watched the hall. From the quays a high-pitched squeal rocketed into the room. Shane fastened his trousers and pulled up his zipper. While buttoning his shirt he walked across the room and pulled apart the heavy red curtains. The reflection of yellow lights disguised the membrane of dirt floating on the river Liffey. About one foot of fake Florentine stucco protruded beneath the window. He pressed his nose against the cold glass and instantly felt it numb. Beneath the fake Florentine stucco he again heard the squeal of brakes as a bus revved up its engine to wheeze its way deeper into the city as if it were on 50 a day.

"You're not going to answer that?"

"Uh-huh," Shane said. He liked the sound of her dubiety.

Shane shut the living-room door and flicked on the hall light. He peeped through the spyhole. With a sigh he opened the door. "Hi, Patrick. Listen man, I don't mean to be a prick but this is a bad time."

"Em Shane . . . look, we've got to talk." Patrick was still in his work clothes. Even in an Italian suit he looked like a binman.

"Bizzzzzzz-eeee, Patrick. Busy. Talk to you tomorrow, OK?"

Patrick squeezed between the door and Shane. His eyes were lowered but his pupils darted around as if trying to catch reality off-guard.

"What is it then?" Shane said, feeling uncomfortable with Patrick's peculiar obstinacy. "Nuala's inside . . . we can't go in there."

"It'll only take a minute," Patrick mumbled.

"Speak up. Can't hear you."

"It'll only . . . I'm quitting. I quit."

Shane's jaw dropped and he then felt ridiculous for letting it do so.

Patrick ran his hands through his thick bush of hair and blushed and swallowed like a man who had just clapped in the wrong place during an arty play.

"You *are* kidding . . . tell me you're kidding."

"No. Look Shane, I'm sorry but –"

"Come on, man, what's the problem? We're mates. We stick by each other. And I know I've been difficult since . . ." Shane paused and considered playing the sympathy card. But he couldn't do it. "I know I've been difficult to work with lately – but we're mates and we work well together. Don't worry about not getting the contract renewed. We'll pull through. Promise. I'm the man. I know I haven't been putting it in lately but I'm back now. I'm back." Shane stared at Patrick. There was a green crust lodged in the corner of one eye and Shane reckoned that Patrick had another eye infection. Guys like Patrick *always* have eye infections.

"I quit. Sorry. Nothing to do with you. I mean . . . I mean that in a nice way. I don't mean it in a mind-your-own-business type of way but I mean it in a way that the reason I'm leaving does not – *is not* because of you. You're great, *bud*. I mean that. And you'll be fine out on your own. Jesus, it'll probably be the biggest mistake of my life but I'm quitting. I want out." Patrick held Shane's gaze. It was becoming clear that Patrick had finally reached the age where he was the man he was always meant to be.

Shane chewed the nail of his forefinger and knew it was over with Patrick. "What have you got lined up?"

"Em . . . nothing really."

"Come on, bud, tell me." Shane smiled in a genuinely-interested-kind-of-way.

"No – nothing." Patrick backed away towards the hall door.

"Come on. You're smarter than that and you know the scene – it'll be embarrassing for me to find out from someone else. You *know* that."

Patrick looked at his feet. He mumbled something. Shane put his hand behind his ear and cocked it forward. "Sorry, little ladybird, didn't catch that."

"Orla. I'm taking the post of artistic dir –"

"You cunt!" Shane shouted. "You *fucking* Judas."

"It's not like that." Patrick leaned his body forward and brushed aside wet strands of hair glued to his forehead.

"You know she's fucked me up." Shane's neck had tensed to a painful level and he snapped his head from side to side to slacken the muscles.

"We'd talked about it before all this. I *promise*, Shane."

"She was lining *you* up before shooting me down. Jesus! You knew that! You cunt. Pretending that you knew nothing in the Morrison Hotel. You fuck."

"Look – I just think . . . I just think she's a genius in her own little way. She knows where she is and where's she's going and –"

Shane was exasperated. He so wanted to hit Patrick. "Genius – that fucking tit?" He palmed Patrick in the chest and Patrick slammed against the wall.

"Come off it, Shane," Patrick said as his eyes rapidly flickered. "You don't occupy the moral high ground here. I mean, come on, you attacked me – literally attacked me – at the Morrison Hotel. Not the type of thing a mate would do. You've become a prick and I don't want to work with you any more. While Orla – Orla rekindled my interest in the whole business."

"You selfish wanker." In an ecstasy of anger Shane slapped Patrick across the face. For a second Patrick was stunned by the sharp sound that resonated through the narrow hall. Shane slapped him again. Short quick flicks of his wrist colliding against Patrick's temple and cheeks and the back of his head. Watching Patrick grunt and moan felt good and Shane was filled with the confidence of knowing when wrong can be the only right. "Cunt. Stupid cunt. Stupid fucking cunt," Shane muttered as he felt his fingers sting and curl inwards and begin to punch. Patrick's arms flailed like a burning man trying to outrun his own burning body. There was a loud clatter and Patrick crumpled to Shane's feet.

"Get off me, you nutter," Patrick shouted from the ground.

Shane fought the urge to kick him in the stomach. It was an open shot. Easy. And it would feel good. "Beg for mercy," Shane whispered. "Beg, you fucking dog."

"You've lost it. You've lost it."

"Are *you* trying to tell *me* something? Are you, telling me, something? You fuck." Shane slapped him again. "You filthy worthless cunt." Slaps rained against the back of Patrick's head, the sides of his arms, anywhere that was flat and open. "Don't *you* tell *me*. Don't you tell me. Don't you tell me!"

"Help," Patrick whimpered. "Get him off me. Help me."

The living-room door was open and Nuala stood there

fully dressed. She was so neat and tidy, she looked as if she'd been born into her white jeans and tee shirt. Shit, Shane thought. How long has she being standing there? How much did she see? She'll be scared and I'll have to calm her down. I could kill Patrick – that stupid fucking cunt.

"You're pathetic," she said with a sneer. She leaned against the door and folded her arms. "You fucking artist's assistant."

"M-m-me?" Patrick said from the ground with a look of horrified awareness.

Nuala approached Shane and placed an arm around his waist. She stared down at the trembling mess. "You're a traitor," Nuala said while squeezing Shane's firm left buttock. "You disgust me. You have all the appeal of a paper cut. You're a fucking leper. A pig."

"You two suit each other," Patrick said and hunched himself against the wall.

Shane flicked his right foot forward and connected with the side of Patrick's nose. It immediately leaked blood and two globs fell onto his yellow tie. They spread until the two foul stains became one.

"Oh Jesus," Patrick shouted. "My nose. My nose."

Shane opened the door and checked the corridor. He then grabbed Patrick by the hair and pulled him forward on all fours. He hated the feel of his greasy hair. Shane wanted to punish him for that too.

"I'm bleeding on my suit," Patrick said to the white floor tiles. "All over the bloody thing. How can I go –"

"Fuck off, Patrick." Shane kicked him again and he fell into a face-down sprawl. "You've thirty seconds to leave the building." Shane shut the door.

Immediately Nuala embraced him from behind. She bit the back of his neck – a wide full bite that was vampirism in its impetus. She licked upwards to his ear lobe, nibbled it and whispered, "That was a . . . a beautiful abduction . . . 'beg like a dog' . . . Jesus, you're an evil boy."

Shane, feeling like a virile invincible gladiator, turned around.

"Uh-oh . . . gotta go," Nuala said while glancing at her watch. She was smiling, calm and ordinary.

"No way." Shane's voice was sulky and he couldn't help it. Nuala had made him feel like a hero and now she was going. He wondered how many fights she'd started over the years, just so she could watch.

"Yeah – up early and all that – things to do."

"What things?"

"The Internet," Nuala admitted while pulling on her jacket that had been hanging over the narrow wooden staircase leading up to the attic bedroom. "Keep an eye from the corridor window in case poxy-Patrick is hovering around the car park. Bye-bye, baby."

"Don't go," Shane muttered while opening the door. "I really . . . really want you to stay. I need you to –"

"You're embarrassing yourself," Nuala said and marched off down the corridor to the alloy doors of the lift.

Chapter Ten

"Unbelievable," Andrew muttered. He was sitting on the sofa staring at a colour picture of a beaked whale in the latest issue of *Cetacean* magazine. At last, he thought, the *Mesoplodon hectori* in the flesh. It was previously only known from skeletons – but lucky, *lucky* Philip Matthews got a snap of it off the coast of New Zealand. And what a beauty she is.

Breakfast TV was on in the background. It was oddly satisfying listening to the neighbours start up their cars at eight to crawl off into the city for the everydayathon. Now, just after nine, the housewives were beginning to pull off in their grey or black space-wagons to be the first in line at the supermarket or hairdresser's or newsagent's.

Andrew had intended to play music but he couldn't find anything he'd wanted to hear. Three separate racks of CDs totalling at least one hundred discs and there was nothing he'd like to play. He remembered the thrill of buying new music – popping the silver disc from its bland plastic holder. Taking satisfaction as daylight sprayed a rainbow onto the shiny surface. But these days he just wanted silence. Or whale noise.

A rapid thudding sounded as Nuala charged down the stairs. He heard her swing around the banister pole and continue to the kitchen. *Click* went the kettle followed by the deep rumbling of the water as it began to warm. Finally the *ba-bing* of the coffee spoon in mid-stir.

Last night Andrew had rooted himself to the kitchen table trying to concentrate on the reproductive strategies of the bowhead whale. Nuala had come home late. "Making-and-doing at Nuala's Moonage Daydream," she'd said. Then she had suggested that he take the following day off. "It would do you good," she'd said, "and we need to talk. You *know* we need to talk." Someone had then phoned. Twice. And each time Nuala had taken it upstairs. They were short phone calls. It was weird because only Rachel, her old school pal and fortnightly swimming partner, ever rang for Nuala.

She entered the living-room wearing loose black slacks and a baggy black tee shirt. It made her look surprisingly fat. Andrew looked up expecting a coffee but she was only holding a single red mug.

"Gee thanks," he said as she sat down on the leather chair.

"Where's the anti-boredom device?" she asked.

Andrew threw her the remote control.

"Die," she said and aimed. The screen went dead and for a second the air was alive with static. Nuala slurped her coffee. "God, why is it that no matter how hard I try, my coffee never comes close to yours?" She slurped again. "Today I'm ordering parcels of ginger over the net from Japan."

"Ginger?" Andrew glanced at his watch. He wondered who would be taking his ten-thirty appointment.

"Yep. Takes about a month to get here and last Christmas, stocks were so low. Hence when the Christmas fashion-flu strikes, I'll be ready to make another killing with my ginger cure. For two weeks of the year Nuala's Moonage Daydream is not just a cosmetic parlour, you know. And who says I don't take my business seriously?" Nuala outstretched her arm and muzzled Andrew with the glare of her palm. "Today *is* an important day. I have something for you."

"You've something for me? I thought you wanted to talk."

"Come – to the bat cave." Nuala breezed from the room. She'd left behind her mug of coffee and its little swirls of steam. Everything was slightly strange and there was nothing strange about that. But Andrew was a believer in the catastrophic view of life – things go along as usual until there's a catastrophe.

He followed her upstairs. Nuala was already plonked on the office chair in front of the computer. The modem was making its high-pitched howl as it plugged her into the World Wide Web.

Andrew checked his watch. Matt was in conference room . . . ten probably. The best thing about Rennes, Saunière & Château was that it was an approximation of certainty.

Nuala whooshed a gust of smoke against the screen. Her right hand clicked the mouse. "Almost there. Give me a profile. Here we are . . . there. Watch ya think?"

Andrew leaned over her shoulder. The screen showed a

perfect quality photograph of a gorgeous blonde young man. He was dressed in black. Black as in American male model and not black as in dangerous dark mystic. He was standing against a redbrick wall looking so uninterested in such an interesting way. "Mmmm, who's that?"

"HornyDub. Just your type, huh?"

"HornyDub? What is it with gorgeous, good-looking dumb Irish guys? They can have whatever they want in this world and inevitably they always choose the damaged woman."

"Damaged woman?" Nuala looked over her shoulder and blew smoke into his face.

Andrew squinted against the smoke. "Is there another kind?" he asked and patted her head.

Nuala shifted from left to right like a weary boxer and said, "Pat-as-in-patronise. Back off. And this guy, HornyDub, is my gift to you. You need cheering up, moping around like a long cold glass of water."

"What? I don't cyber. I've never cybered and I . . . Jesus, if that's what I've taken a day off work for –"

"Relax, Andrew, my dear brother." Nuala swivelled on the business chair. "Everything is taken care of. Look at it as a thank-you for all those yummy pasta dishes and the fact that your little outburst the night Shane was here . . . what was it you'd said? 'Decadence to me was a condom before I moved in with you'? Well you can take satisfaction from the fact that that *did* rankle. And now I'm showing you how fucking right-on and cool I am and you – you're going to have an extraordinary walk in the park today."

"Today? In the park?" Andrew examined the picture of HornyDub. He leaned forward and brushed Nuala's hand off the mouse. He pointed and clicked. The computer magnified HornyDub's eyes. They were blue. A wonderful type of blue. A young-Liam type of blue. "He's bent? What's he doing wasting his time with you?"

"He's – a free spirit. Game for a laugh and for me he'll do *anything*. He wants to try it. You'll like HornyDub. He's in his element. He has been for about two years now. Don't let him down."

* * *

Friday's traffic had ground to a halt right on time. Andrew didn't mind though. The blind date in the park had lightened his mood and the sun was hot and his elbow leaned out the window of his black BMW. It was the type of day that made the junkies on O'Connell Street look healthy. He lowered his shades and fingered the CDs scattered across the passenger seat: Abba, Chemical Brothers, 80's Bowie, and Robbie Williams. Since the window was open he picked the Chemical Brothers. The bass pounded and treated guitars melded and heads wearily turned in the surrounding cars. Music was vital again.

"*Hey boys* . . . why aren't we moving? *Superstar DJs* . . . *here we go*!" He played drums on the steering wheel. Up ahead was a bottleneck kamikaze junction spilling onto the coast road. The man in a battered blue Volvo climbed out, raised his hand over his eyes and stared down the road like a desert general. Then he slapped the roof of his car. Andrew pressed 'pause'. Other people were leaning out their windows and scanning ahead. Something had happened.

His mobile bleeped. Andrew clicked free his seat belt and picked up the little phone. "Yeah?"

"Been looking for ya, man."

"Who is it?"

"That *fucking* bitch you share your blood with – Nora – kept saying 'wrong number' and hanging up."

"Liam?" Andrew checked his watch. He had fifteen minutes to get to the park. He cursed himself for taking the coast road.

"All last night – well, about twice. And this morning it was just engaged. Engaged, engaged, engaged. Tried your mobile too but it was off. Didn't want to leave a message because of our . . . *situation*."

"What do you want?" Andrew had a colour printout of HornyDub resting on his lap. He wondered if the clothes were designer.

"And it's not as if I had better things to be doing," Liam continued. He paused for a moment and Andrew heard the rolling flint of a lighter. Liam took a drag of his cigarette and cleared his throat.

Andrew clicked open the car door and stepped outside. The hot air was full of growling fumes and he held the phone to his head aware of everyone's stare and of every muscular movement in his body.

About ten cars ahead a group were crouched and silent.

Andrew unbuttoned his jacket and moved between the stalled grumbling cars. He stopped when he was only ten feet away from the crouched group. At the centre of their attention was a body. Andrew dropped the mobile phone to his side. It was so hot. "An ambulance *is* on its way, yes?" he asked. Four faces looked up. They seemed numb and lifeless, like dead bodies shielding a bleeding one. There was a mother with a scarf tied around her hair and a yellow shopping bag beside her. There were two professional males in cheap everyday suits.

One of the professionals was pale and trembling and was obviously *the* driver. Finally there was a priest. He was young and pale and looked hopeless as if only beginning to realise that he was just another failed version of the Son of God.

Andrew raised the phone to his ear. Liam was in mid-spiel. Andrew moved forward like he was approaching a dangerous animal. The priest was making the sign of the cross above the dying head like the slash-slash of a Jedi light-sabre. Andrew loved it when they did that. He wanted to look away in much the same way he'd want to turn off an excellent horror movie. To stay was the thrill, the point. "I'm hanging up now," he whispered.

"No wait, man! I was talking to Blofeldt."

"What? When?" Andrew looked up to the sky. Dark blue and so non-Irish.

"Yesterday. Listen. He says he sent it to you."

"No, he didn't."

"Yeah, Andy. He swears. Sent it years ago. He's presumed you've had it all this time. Either that or got rid of it."

"Trust me," Andrew whispered. "He's lying." Andrew hung up. The priest, still crouched on the ground, was looking up at him as if he would take considerable pleasure in sentencing the likes of Andrew to heaven.

Andrew couldn't see what the victim was wearing. He couldn't even tell how old he was. There was just an unblemished face cradled in the priest's arms. His beady eyes were squeezed and glistening. Tears expanded like living entities and deflated their way down his cheek. Then his eyes blinked and Andrew was so riveted by the view that he felt cheated of a second.

Andrew's elbow hit against the side mirror of a red

Volkswagen Polo. Immediately a twenty-something blonde honked her horn and exclaimed from her open window, "Hey, what do you think you're doing?"

Andrew ignored her and stared over the steaming river of stalled sepulchral machines.

"Can you fix my mirror, please?" the blonde said and smirked beneath a confident stare that could not quite smother the origins of her north-side Dublin accent.

Andrew looked through her windscreen and observed how the givers of life were no longer interested in the living. "No," Andrew replied and thought of HornyDub and his smile grew and beamed until it felt like a thousand people applauding inside his head.

* * *

"Come on," Shane hissed over the steering wheel. "Get him off the . . . who is *that* guy?"

Three cars in front of him a man was standing in the middle of the stalled traffic. He looked in complete control, like a hero, like someone who would like to save a life. He was dressed in a nice dark suit and although Shane couldn't see his face, he could presume the guy was handsome owing to his thick black groomed hair, slim build and consequential gait. He was living proof of how some people would always be more equal than others.

The guy vanished down the tunnel of cars in the opposite direction and nothing of interest remained besides the car crash. Shane craned his neck out the window. A man was on the ground surrounded by a priest and pedestrians. Shane squinted. There wasn't much to see. The priest was muttering in the man's ear, as if explaining how

God does terrible things to people and then waits for them to ask for forgiveness.

Shane was late. Nuala had called him twenty minutes ago and told him that there was an emergency – that she needed to see him *now*. Shane checked the dashboard clock and muttered, "Fuck".

The victim's hand rested against the killing machine's bumper and there was an indentation beneath the flesh, as if he'd left a handprint in mercury. There was no blood. Violence, it seemed, was better on TV than on the streets.

There was a sharp loud noise. His elbow had accidentally hit the horn. A few drivers glanced at him and then quickly away. It was hot. His throat was dry and the exhaust fumes gathered like phlegm and did not blow away.

Up ahead there was a murmur in the air. Shane turned his engine off. The priest was leading the killer, the killer's friend and the housewife in prayer.

"I'm late," Shane muttered and tried to fathom Nuala's emergency. As the air filled with a shrill blue noise, a fever came over Shane like he was falling down a hole where no one could follow. In this packed metal-logged street he felt an isolation vaster than Russia. Shane stared ahead through the shimmering heat and past the crash to where the sun hung over the city. It would be nice to stare at that star until something interesting emerged.

* * *

Nuala watched Shane watch his feet. He was sitting in the middle of the leather sofa where Andrew would sit. He clutched a glass of Andrew's favourite Chardonnay and Nuala couldn't help but feel it was wasted on him.

"My emergency is later," Nuala said. "First look." She gestured to some black-framed prints of whales hanging on the walls. "Bet you feel at home, huh?"

"Indifferent wall-fodder," Shane said to his crossed knees and went red. Sometimes Nuala found his overawed timidity annoying rather than flattering.

"Yeah – Andrew picked them. Here, I've got something to show you. Something *I* picked up a long time ago. Well, a few years ago anyway. You were probably still at college." Nuala crossed the room and crouched down beside the black metal stereo cabinet. She reached behind and pulled out a rolled poster that had been jammed against the wall. "Now this is not 'indifferent wall-fodder'," Nuala said with a smile. She stood in the middle of the room and unfurled the poster like she was making a presentation. It was a perfect picture of a blown-up photograph. A brick wall was painted white with a blue neon sign electrifying the message – MY CUNT IS WET WITH FEAR.

Shane glanced at it and drained the wine glass dry with a squint of disrelish.

"What you think, Shane? A rare cool radical feminist statement?"

Shane smirked. "Now that you mention it – I can suddenly see it in the artist's oeuvre. Look Nuala, to be honest, I've always *hated* Tracey Emin."

"How did you know it was Tracey –"

"Because I sold a million copies of that to a million *Guardian*-reader versions of you. What do you want to know about? Her botched abortion? Her rape? The dimensions of her boyfriend's dick? Her suicide attempts? I can tell you. I know everything about Turner Prize nominees. Big money spinner at Hieronymus Bosch."

"Well, aren't you fucking great," Nuala muttered and dropped the poster behind the black leather chair. Then she muttered, "Emin is an art-flasher."

"Art-flasher," Shane repeated. "That's good. That's the type of bullshit I used to hear from Patrick. And I don't have Patrick around any more. I don't have a business any more either. And quite soon I won't have any more money. Oh God, I am so fucked."

Nuala flicked her fringe and then ran her hands roughly through the rest of her hair. "For fuck's sake, Shane, grow up! You know . . . when I saw you standing poetically in the water on Almond Beach watching the sunset disappear, I thought –"

"Poetically?" Shane went red again and lowered his head.

"Yeah – you looked awful that night. A complete wanker. I reckoned you were either a sensitive prick that couldn't find a forest to cry in or a suicide. That's why I spoke to you. And it was really disappointing that you weren't a suicide-type-of-guy. I've so much admiration for those who top themselves. Especially intelligent people. They work it out. They figure life out. And they make a decision. They make a decision with a sword. It's a brave insightful thing to do."

"With a sword?" Shane said and looked bewildered.

"It's a *tarot*-thing. Anyway you're cowardly and bunny-rabbit-like. Since when – and I'm not talking about today – since when did you think you had a future anyway? Things are very simple, Shane. Nothing matters. Nothing. And the more you think about it, the more complicated nothing becomes. It's like – it's like when I brought Mam to the hospital for a throat infection a few months ago. We were walking around these *Death Star* corridors looking for the 'ear, nose and throat department'. Some nurse pointed us on our way. 'It's clearly signposted', she said. I said, 'No, it isn't'. She then sighed like the asshole all medical people are and pointed to a sign. Know what it read? It read, 'otorhinolaryngology department' and then an arrow pointing this way." Nuala pointed with a thumb over her shoulder. "It's like Nuala's Moonage Daydream. I used to order dead wood from Germany for certain top-secret back-room projects. Two years ago they wrote asking if I'd meant 'coarse woody debris'. Last year they'd changed that into the abbreviation 'CWD'. And, get this, just a few weeks ago they wrote again to inform me that the 'European Union publications on the natural environment' have ordered that CWD is now to be referred to as 'necromass'. Fucking necromass! Just give me some dead wood, please."

Nuala knelt down on the rug in front of him. She placed her hands over his. He always looked so wanting but uncertain of how to ask for it. She imagined a rusty sharp bolt out of place in his stomach. Nuala squeezed his hands. "Shane, what are we to each other? I thought – I presumed – that we were a team. We're lovers. I mean I know we've not . . . made love. But we *are* lovers, right? And . . . and something more than that. We trust each other. You trusted me and, today, I'm going to return that trust by putting you in the same situation. We've got to trust each other. You do know I'd do anything for you? *Anything*." Nuala reached forward and gripped Shane by the chin. She lifted his head and stared into his green eyes. There was a twitch of a smile at the corners of his lips, and Nuala could see that he never wanted to find the ordinary again.

"Shane, come upstairs to my room. Fuck me slowly. Don't talk. Just rock in and out . . . I reckon now is the time."

"The time?" Shane swallowed as if he was three seconds away from taking the stage.

"Yeah," Nuala said. She was finished being a virgin.

Nuala sat on the side of the bed. She was naked and her breasts felt flabby. Shane lay the length of the bed, a single sheet covering him. His feet and ankles stuck out and Nuala liked the light coating of hair over his smooth skin.

"Your bedroom," Shane said to the ceiling, "is so ordinary."

Nuala scanned the room. Ordinary? she thought. It's just a bedroom. What was a bedroom supposed to be? Two wardrobes, a handbasin, dresses and skirts draped on hangers suspended from doors, a little framed family photograph including dead-dad, a Walkman for when she borrowed Andrew's night-time-whale-sounds and a scattering of CD-ROMs that hadn't made it to the computer next door or the bin downstairs. Oh and three ashtrays and patches of tar-brown on the white ceiling.

"That was amazing," Shane calmly stated.

"It was OK." Nuala had liked sexual intercourse. Shane had entered her easily. She'd just started her period and he'd slid in. She'd waited for the pain and had hoped it would be a nice pain. But there was just the sense of being filled in a tingling type of way. And then they'd fucked just like she'd requested. Him lying behind her and she, looking at the daylight and the slate rooftops of houses across the road. She'd liked the way he'd had to cease rocking every ten seconds to stop himself from coming. And she'd liked his smell. The aroma emanated from his armpits and chest. It wasn't sickly or stale. She remembered when she was ten and had hated boys. She'd thought that they were animals that sweated in all weathers.

"Perfect," Shane said.

"It was OK," Nuala repeated. She thought of her periods and how she'd never ever use a tampon. Nothing man-made will ever kill me, Nuala thought. There's no way I'd ever put anything with an artificial fibre called rayon into my flower. I know all about toxic shock – comes with the territory. Pity Lisa never knew me. I'm sure we would have hated each other.

Nuala pulled back Shane's blanket and said, "Rise and shine, soldier – you've got to deal with my emergency."

Shane careered around suburban corners in his silver Ford Puma with Nuala sitting rigid beside him. Nuala's silence irritated him. Shane thought of Lisa and wondered if that was what Nuala was thinking about. He wondered if she considered him guilty. She hadn't mentioned it since he'd told her about the tampon. Not a word.

Nuala sniffed the air. "You got your car cleaned."

Immediately Shane felt his cheeks and his cock fill with blood. He quickly nodded before screeching to a halt beside the park wall overlooking the pond.

Nuala leaned across the gear stick and raised his wrist and illuminated the watch's blue digital face. "I hope you haven't changed your mind. It's just fun, yeah?"

"No. Jesus, no way." Shane kissed her forehead and Nuala pulled away. She quickly threw him a wink.

They walked down a wheelchair-friendly concrete ramp,

which turned into a pathway leading to the pond. Even though it was three in the afternoon it was still very hot. Shane licked his lips and thought of a Coke.

He took advantage of lighting a cigarette to glance at Nuala. She looked straight ahead with her pink shades. Her loose black tee shirt was tucked into her black slacks to show off her waist. The peak of her baseball cap was turned upwards to allow the sun on her factor-fifteen protected face. "That's the shit thing about Ireland," Nuala mumbled pensively, "you've got to create your own – I dunno – Eros stuff, I suppose. Now a walk in New York's Central Park or even the park in London on a day like today would give any voyeur enough material for –"

"You're so," Shane began and swallowed for air, "you're so fucking dirty." His cock was hard and he wanted to tell her this but he didn't have the nerve.

Nuala smiled. "Even in a heatwave like this there will never be an Irish cailín playing on a beach in Kerry or Cork or even knackville Bray in a string bikini."

Shane laughed and wished he'd brought his shades. They weren't in his car. Where the fuck were they? Expensive too – black Ray-Bans. He could no longer afford to lose such things.

The sun disappeared behind a leafy canopy of broad deciduous leaves. The shadow that blanketed them was green and cool. That was something that art had taught Shane – shadow wasn't always black. The dead leaves on the ground had been there for months and when Shane stood on them they turned to dust rather than crunched. He fastened the top button of his shirt and was aware that he was breathing heavily even though he wasn't out of breath.

"This way," Nuala said and turned off the concrete path onto a dry muck-track that vermiculated into the thick undergrowth. "And from here in, let's keep it quiet."

Nuala reckoned that walking through the long grass and sticky bramble slowed time. No – it changed time. Like what several generations of space flight would do. Mankind isn't built to float. It depressed Nuala that the outer reaches of the galaxy are unreachable even in a spaceship with a limitless fuel supply. A small confined population of space pioneers would be subject to extreme inbreeding, she thought. And then after a few generations you would lose your feet. Instead of arms and legs you would have just four arms – more useful in microgravity. The space pioneers would also eventually lose their distance vision and their hearing because there's nothing to see outside the windows and nothing to hear. Nuala looked at her feet – *crack, snap, crack*, go the dead branches. Nuala took a deep breath. Up ahead was a rugged hill festooned with the chunky roots of huge fat oak trees. Nuala thought of the space pioneers – generations down the line when they eventually reach a habitable planet, they would hit the ground with a splat, barely able to move against gravity's normal pull, crawling on all fours, blind, deaf and inbred – the hillbillies of the universe.

"We need wormholes," Nuala muttered and plucked a thick wooden log from the ground.

"Huh, worms?" Shane stopped and looked around his feet.

"*Quiet*, I said."

At the top of the small hill Nuala led the way. She

crouched and threw back a cautionary hand. Slowly they moved forward, the log swinging by Nuala's side. They were far away from the main pathways, which encircled the park with prams, roller-blades and bicycles. The only noises were the shuffle of dead leaves, magpies up in the trees and the odd bee chugging by.

"We're here," Nuala whispered. She felt her heart pound and thought of ten thousand expended cigarettes.

"Where?" Shane whispered and crouched down beside her.

They were in the middle of the wood. The trees grew into each other in a chaotic spray of seed dispersion. Grey branches coiled about one another but seemed solid and dry and not at all supple and volatile like rope. But the green vegetation was sparse and Nuala had already spotted them.

"There they are." Nuala pointed.

"Where . . . oh yeah." Shane was panting heavily and he covered his mouth with his hands to contain the noise.

About twenty feet ahead were mutterings and the sharp crack of branches. Through the translucent web of dead dry branches Nuala could see the back of Andrew's broad straight suit. In front of him was the smaller HornyDub. She could see his blond hair peeking over Andrew's right shoulder and occasionally his short-sleeved arm took an arc-shaped route to his mouth as he puffed on a cigarette.

Nuala remembered creeping down the stairs in the dead of night when she was supposed to be fast asleep. She'd bundle herself at the living-room door and listen to her parents and friends laughing and eating and drinking. It had outraged her that Andrew was allowed stay up. Then she'd wake back in her bed with no idea of how she'd got there and by the time she'd come down for breakfast she'd already forgotten about it all.

Nuala looked at the ground and gently swept her palm before her feet. Dry and crispy with no creepy things like the Tarantula Hawk Wasp hiding beneath the brown leaves. She knelt down.

"This isn't as exciting as I thought it would be," Shane muttered.

Nuala sighed. Shane was bugging her. It was a pity his presence was necessary. "We're here for insight and knowledge," Nuala said and reached back to shoo away a groping hand from her ass.

"I thought we were going to . . . you know . . . have fun?"

Ahead in the clearing there was low laughter as a small scuffle broke out. Nuala sniffed. The air was ripe with pleasant sulphur and a lazy aftertaste of smoke. She withdrew her cigarette box and after flipping it open, sucked one out with her lips. "Light," she mumbled and tapped the ground with her forefinger. Shane rifled his pockets. Finally a flame lit the tip of her cigarette. Nuala inhaled and said, "Shane, I'm still far from understanding the meaning of life. But today progress has been made: I'm now confused at a higher level."

"Hey . . . Jesus, come back."

Nuala was moving. Twigs brushed through her hair and snagged and Nuala's impetus tore them from their branches. Time was moving too fast to time her heartbeat. Instead she focused on the tiny hairs on her wrist which savoured each momentous pound of her pulse.

She'd made it to the clearing. Nuala could see feet. Doc Marten boots. Oxblood and they seemed to rise and rise until baggy combats conquered them. The combats were ripped on the left knee and then they were bunched about a pair of tanned hairless smooth young thighs. Andrew's opened black trousers and hanging belt buckle blocked the sight of HornyDub's spread buttocks. HornyDub was sandwiched against the tree and grunting hard like the anchorman in a tug of war. Andrew's thrusting black-suited hips froze in time. He turned around. There was a cock. Long and hard but beginning to droop. It had skin covering its top and it gathered in wrinkles where the little slit should have been. That was real foreskin. Real as in not marble and not in Florence behind glass. It was huge and had veins. A black bush of hair barged out around it. Four fingers and a thumb suddenly shook it like it was alive. Drops of moisture ripped loose and disappeared into the shadows.

"Hi," Nuala said and dropped the log she'd been holding to the ground.

Andrew was covering himself and frowning and staring to the ground and thinking hard. Nuala pictured his brain behind that smooth forehead. A hundred electric impulses of what-to-do-next fighting for selection.

"Nuala?" was all he could manage.

Nuala caught herself searching her own brain for a reply and now wished that she could control real time – slow it down until she could feel the stretch of a nanosecond. When Nuala had first learned that a nanosecond was one billionth of a second, her amazement had faded to depression. There was so much time to waste. A second ticks and there goes a billion nanoseconds.

"Nuala?" Andrew repeated. Bewilderment overtook his disbelief.

But Nuala's grail lay in the proven measurement of the

femtosecond. A femtosecond, she thought, was for some reason the most appeasing fact in the world. So what if there is no God because *there is* a femtosecond. A femtosecond is a millionth of a nanosecond – an actual sequence of time measured only with gas and lasers. One day they'll divide a femtosecond into a million different parts and discover . . . what?

"Andy?" HornyDub was pulling up his combats. "What's going . . . Supergirl!" He staggered forward from the tree, giggling and loose-limbed.

"Nuala?" Andrew said again. His composure had returned and he ran his hand through thick hair.

"It's Nuala!" HornyDub shouted and tripped and fell to the forest floor at Andrew's feet. "Knew it was something cool like Tanya but thought it was Nuala. What did I just say?" Lying outstretched on the ground he covered his mouth and started laughing.

"What are you doing? I mean, like, here?" Andrew dusted his black jacket.

Nuala gazed down at HornyDub. He looked about fourteen lying on the ground, going red as he tried to contain his laughter while at the same time inching his head towards Nuala's boots to try and see up the baggy legs of her trousers. "What's up with him?"

"Mark's on his first trip. He's a virgin – as you promised – so I gave him a Mitsubishi to ease things for him."

"For *you*, you mean." Nuala stared into Andrew's brown eyes. Today was one of those days that she didn't like their colour. There was too much necromass about.

Mark pulled himself up into a hunched position. "I'm not . . . I'm not a virgin any more," he panted.

"Snap," Nuala muttered.

Andrew's eyes widened and he stepped away from Nuala. "Shane!"

"Em, yeah," Shane said as he winced his way through the remaining branches which protected the rim of the clearing.

Andrew turned to Nuala and broadly smiled. "Jesus, Nuala, you've pushed the boat out this time. You are . . . you are the weirdest of people. But a gem of a sister nonetheless."

Nuala watched Shane stretch himself to full height. He made a spitting sound as his fingers tugged at invisible spider strands around his lips.

Andrew smiled. "So Shane's game for a laugh too?"

"Huh?" Shane said in the background, only half-listening.

Nuala shrugged.

"This is so cool," Andrew said. "Hey, Shane. Feeling more comfortable with – with yourself now?"

Shane looked with astonishment at the scene laid out before him. "Huh?" he said again and stared down at the hunched and still giggling Mark.

"Talk to him," Nuala whispered to Andrew.

Andrew beamed and whispered, "I'd prefer if you didn't – you know – hang around in the long term."

"I know," said Nuala. She bent down to Mark. "So HornyDub, you're Mark."

"Told you that, when we met at the pond."

"Wasn't listening to you."

"I know – you were weird then. So I did what you commanded, Supergirl. And it hurt." Mark's smile grew to a laugh. Then he said, "But it hurt so good!"

Nuala raised a finger before her lips and whispered, "Quiet, Mark. Shhhh."

"OK. Now it's your turn. This is so fucking cool. You make . . . you make dreams come true. I've dreamt about shit like this. Jesus, you are so sexy. I mean that. Look, my hand is shaking. Let's do all the shit we've ever spoken about. Let's do it. Come on, Supergirl. Come on." Mark slowly rose from his hunches.

"You don't know . . . what you're dealing with," Nuala whispered while holding his stare.

Behind her Shane was laughing awkwardly at something Andrew had said. "No way," Shane stated. "Not a chance. You've got the wrong end of the stick here, pal."

Andrew sounded less certain. "But – but I don't understand."

"What are you talking about?" Mark said, still smiling in white and flushed with health like a young Nazi poster boy.

"They're going to kill you," Nuala whispered.

"What?" Mark blinked his stoned glazed blue eyes but his smile remained. He neurotically licked his huge red lips.

"Look," Nuala whispered and gestured to her stomach. Mark lowered his gaze. Nuala had opened the waist button to her trousers. She pulled out her tee-shirt and showed off her pierced belly-button.

"Cool," Mark said and wiped his lips with the back of his hand.

Nuala's fingers walked down her belly to the rim of her plain white cotton panties. She checked on Andrew and Shane over her shoulder. They were still in awkward conversation.

"Mark," Nuala whispered, "you're fucking dead." She

shoved her fingers down the front of her panties. "So dead." Nuala was barely audible. She withdrew her hand from between her legs and rubbed her fingers across her pierced belly. Four streaks of dark menstrual blood trailed her fingers. "Run," Nuala growled and pushed him in the chest. Her head jutted forward and she glared like she'd glare at her executioner.

"Jesus fucking Christ," Mark mumbled in a suppressed high-pitch. His eyes rapidly blinked and he tore his gaze from Nuala's midriff to the two men behind her. He turned and barged into the wood, not even using his hands to swipe aside the branches.

"What the . . ." Andrew was beside her, staring after Mark.

"He's flipped. Off his head," Nuala said. "Shane, go and find him. Andrew, what did you give him?"

"Just a –"

"Shane," Nuala shouted. "Go!"

"For fuck's sake," Shane muttered before jogging past them and into the forest, careful to avoid the leafless grey branches veering towards his face.

"A Mitsubishi," Andrew said. "Just a Mitsubishi." Scratching his head he gazed after the zigzagging fading shape of Shane. His legs spread and he cast aside the flaps of his jacket like the man he was, with a high-powered job. "This is a strange day, Nuala," Andrew said, still staring into the forest.

"Yeah," Nuala said. She bent over and picked up the log lying at her feet. She smashed the log down onto the back of Andrew's skull.

Andrew leaned forward at an odd precarious angle. His

hands raised to cover his head, his fingers interlinking just above the back of his neck. He slowly turned to face Nuala, who was still leaning forward and slightly bent. His eyes were squeezed and struggling to focus as if Nuala had just pulled him out of bed.

"Nuala," he whispered, "what are you doing to me?"

Nuala felt the weight of the thick log raised for the second time above her head. She swung the log downwards. Andrew lowered his head. The log whacked against the back of his skull and Nuala felt something like an electric shock in her hands. A hairline crack appeared down the centre of the log. Andrew dropped to the ground. His arms spread as if he'd been just fired into the earth. He was still.

Chapter Eleven

Shane swiped a clasping twig from his hair. He felt moisture beneath his left armpit. He hated being sweaty. "Hey," he shouted, "Mark!"

"Fuck off!" the blond teenager shouted from ten feet in front.

"Fine then," Shane muttered and was about to gladly give up when there was a loud whack. Shane jogged to a standstill and stared down at the bleeding face of Mark. He was outstretched on the ground, arms spread, trousers still undone, nose crooked and smeared with blood from its collision with a tree.

"Moron," Shane muttered. He tapped the side of Mark's face. "Hello? Come on. You there?"

Mark groaned and his head slowly moved from side to side.

"You ran into a tree. Just relax." Shane heard voices. He knelt beside Mark and squinted ahead. The foliage was thick and green but twenty feet away there was a concrete-carving drone as roller-blades sped by on the pathway.

"I'll be back with Nuala," Shane whispered. He didn't like the idea of hiding in bushes with drugged-up queers. Once again he crashed through the dehydrated knot of branches until the clearing opened up before him.

"What's up, Nuala . . . Andy?" Shane said and made a perplexed face towards the outstretched body on the ground.

Nuala was standing over Andrew, the log hanging by her side, one knee bent and an awkward smile. Shane walked over to Nuala and said, "Houston, we've got a problem. Mark has knocked himself out. Hey, Andy?" Shane tapped his foot against Andrew's hip. He didn't move. Shane looked at Nuala. "Is he fucked-up too?" Shane wiped his brow. All this running and drama had made him sticky. He wanted to go home and shower.

"You'd better look at Andrew," Nuala said and turned her head upward to sniff at the high green leaves. "I don't want to see him any more."

"What are you talking about?" Shane shrugged his impatience. He hoped Mark was OK. Concussion can fuck people up for a day or two, he thought. And Mark looked like a guy who still lived with his parents. They'd want to know what happened. Jesus, in a worst-case scenario the cops would be involved. I'm going home.

"I'm going home," Shane said. "This is too freaky. Coming? If not, Andy can drive you home. Andy – get up off the fucking ground."

"Look at him," Nuala said and walked over to the trees. She stretched and slapped her palm against the bark. Her other hand swung the log back and forth like a pendulum.

Shane looked down on Andrew. Face in the dirt. Legs

slightly parted. Nice black leather shoes – fresh, grip-less heels. Jacket collar turned up. One hand trapped beneath the weight of his chest. The other hand angled backward and resting on the rear of his head. Dark blood. Not free-flowing. Gluey, pasty. As if it were already congealing between the fingers. As if the fingers were transforming themselves into fleshy fins.

"What's happened?" Shane said but didn't look at Nuala. There was a weight in his chest. He knelt down and lifted the angled hand from the back of Andrew's head. A patch of his thick black hair seemed liquefied. It was a gooey pool of red tar. "Andy?" he whispered. "Andy?" Shane touched the wound with his forefinger. Wet and warm. He pushed a little and instead of skull, there was a squelch and a bubble popped beside his fingertip. "Christ, what the fuck –"

"Oh, shut up," Nuala said and walked forward, holding out the log like an Olympic torch. "I hit him. Hit him twice. Smack, smack – in the same place. Now he's dead. I killed him. I . . . I'm dealing with it. Can you? You'll have to. We're in this . . . don't make me say it."

"This is freaky," Shane said and stood up. He knocked the log from her hand. His heart was pounding. His heart was in his head and he covered his ears with his palms. "I can't believe you've done –" Shane's whisper rose in pitch until he knew that if he said another word it would be a scream.

"Yeah, I did," Nuala said and kicked Andrew's pliant ankle. "Oh look at you! Stop making fucking faces. Deal with it. Be a man! Christ. Pull yourself together . . . look at yourself."

Shane had turned away from Nuala and the body. He

was looking into the woods where Mark lay somewhere. Or maybe he was gone. Gone home to tea. There was a voice in his ears. "God, God, God," it said and it grew louder as he looked away from the depth of the forest and up to the leaves and the cerulean sky hiding above the green. "God, God, God," Shane said, mantra-like. There was a sting of pain across his cheek. Something was holding his elbow, turning him around, positioning him inches from Nuala's face. She was calm except for her eyes. They were wide and a crappy blue and they moved left and right and up and down with the edginess of someone who was caught.

"You're fucking pathetic," she whispered. "*Pathetic*. Deal with it. You're with me in this." She paused to suck the soft flesh at the base of her thumb. Then she continued. This time louder. "'God, God, God' – is that all you can say? Don't tell me you're getting a trendy rush of faith? You prick! You little *fucking* prick!"

"Where are my cigarettes?" he muttered, checking and rechecking the same four empty pockets in his jacket and trousers. "I dropped them in the forest. Mark's unconscious. I want to go. Get me *out* of here." Shane gripped Nuala by the shoulders. "Mark hit a fucking tree. Straight into it. He's lying on the ground bleeding and you – you've killed your fucking brother!" He looked up to the leafy canopy until a breeze shifted the green expanse and he glimpsed another instant of blue. He lowered his gaze to Nuala and forced himself to laugh. "You're fucking mad. Where did . . . how did . . . Jesus!"

Nuala tapped Andrew's ankle with her foot. Softly – until his slightly parted legs closed. "Listen carefully," she said and hunched down beside her brother.

"Uh-huh," Shane said and placed his hand on his chest. His heart was pounding. He flexed his left hand. The left arm is the one where a heart attack sends pangs of sharp pain through it, he thought. Or was it the right arm? He thought of that guy he'd known at college – the one who keeled over dead after a line of coke.

"You killed your girlfriend," Nuala said while pulling Andrew's body over onto its back. "You killed Lisa. Not directly. But you made her wear tampons. I killed my brother, directly. End result – same thing. So we're in this together. We can deal with it. All that whimpering – it's fear and guilt and you don't even know what you're guilty about. That's where we are right now. The 21st century is all about making us feel guilty about not feeling guilty any more. So . . ." Nuala managed to turn the body. Andrew's face was already pale. The lips were blue. Suddenly Andrew coughed. His eyes flicked and he whispered something.

Nuala stared into her brother's face. Her lips moved with silent words. Then she looked up to Shane and said, "So . . . so I'm lying. He's alive. Badly wounded but alive. Gave him a bashing with a log but he's OK. Some stitches needed. Perhaps concussion . . ." Nuala slapped her brother's face. *Whack. Whack.*

Andrew groaned and gurgled and then whimpered. His eyelids had small spasms and then slightly parted.

"Oh, thank Christ," Shane exclaimed and instinctively blessed himself for the first time in almost a decade. "Thank you, God. Thank you. Thank you." His eyes watered and each intake of air felt like a mouthful of the finest food.

Andrew whispered into Nuala's ear. Nuala said, "Andrew, can you walk?"

"Yeah . . . I will be . . . yeah, sure." By way of confirmation he retracted both his legs and then stretched them out again.

Nuala shoved a folded yellow page into Andrew's inner wallet pocket. "Don't read that yet. Wait until you've checked yourself into hospital . . . wait until they've fixed you up. You need to be clear. Understand?"

"Yeah . . . yeah. Thanks, Noodles."

Shane backed away to the edge of the clearing. "He's fucked up, Nuala. Talking shite. He needs an ambulance . . . what the fuck have you done?" Shane regretted saying anything. He wanted to go. Get whatever was going to happen next over and done with.

"Let's go," Nuala said and hooked her arm through Shane's. She led the way through the undergrowth until they were standing on an overgrown ridge at the edge of the forest. The pond spread out below them and roller-bladders whizzed by. Father and son kicked a ball on the grass near Shane's car.

They half-jogged down the dry muck path towards the pond. Shane kept his gaze on Nuala's hand clutching his elbow. It was pale against the black of his jacket.

"Good shot," the father shouted. Shane turned his head. Two bunched jackets acted as goalposts.

"Saved!" the boy roared and the father threw himself to the ground in a display of brawny abhorrence.

There was a hand rooting in Shane's jacket pocket. Nuala found the keys and plugged them into the driver's door of the Puma. It popped open with a throb of warm air.

Behind Shane and on the other side of the wall there was a shriek as the boy saved another goal.

"Get in," Nuala said. "I'm driving."

Nuala drove. Shane sat beside her. Nuala turned on the radio. A talk-show host lectured a dishonest electrician. She turned it off. She turned it on again and browsed the music channels. She turned it off. She turned it on again and Shane's fist punched the dial inwards and off.

She pulled into the driveway. The façade of Andrew's house drew closer like a child's drawing of a big happy face. Shane got out. Nuala followed and thought the sky was blue and lovely.

Richard's wife, Samantha, was on the other side of the fence. Nuala despised her. A forty-something blonde who had clearly married money a long time ago but had never educated herself to it. Too much everything – colour, make-up, volume.

"Hi, Nuala," Samantha said and blushed. "And this is?" Samantha nodded to Shane who was standing in the porch and staring into the distorted bubbled-glass of the front door.

"That's – a friend. Just a friend. No juicy gossip there, I'm afraid."

Samantha swallowed and went a deeper shade of red.

"See ya, Samantha."

"Relax, Shane," Nuala said as she sat into the single leather chair. "Andrew wasn't so nice. He was a sneaky bitch in his own way."

"I don't care," Shane mumbled. He sat on the leather

sofa with his elbows propped on his knees. His hands clasped the side of his head like a young man watching his team get hammered.

"Of course you care," Nuala said in a voice usually reserved for old ladies in Nuala's Moonage Daydream.

Shane leaned back into the sofa and inhaled. "I care that I left a queer unconscious in the woods. I care that you nearly beat your own brother to death. I care that I told you about Lisa. But I can assure you, that *I-do-not-fucking-care* if Andy was nice or not." Shane's hands were folded over his stomach. He was taking short sharp breaths.

"You need to calm down," Nuala said and thought, I wonder why Mam doesn't like Shane. She cleared her throat of whispers and added, "Incidentally I'm not mentally unstable, you know?"

"Oh, Jesus," Shane mumbled.

The curtains were drawn and Shane was totally focused on the video playing on the TV screen. He couldn't believe what he was seeing and hearing. The camera was on a young Andrew. He was in the back of a car looking edgy and mean. An American voice was speaking off camera. It said, "Look, he's a kid. He's eleven. He just looks sixteen . . . the magic of shitty lighting and heavy make-up. Big fucking deal, yeah? Kids are like Pringles. Once you pop them, you can't stop."

Andrew stared from inside the TV and into the darkened living-room. Then he started to laugh. "Great . . . a kid . . . I'm good with kids." Suddenly the footage ended with a rush of interference.

"He's a pedo," Shane said in the darkness of the drawn blinds.

"Uh-huh," Nuala said, from the other side of the room while blowing a ring of smoke.

Shane observed the side profile of Nuala's face. He liked her chubby cheeks. They were a vague tone of red. Her ears were small. He hadn't noticed that before. But the hanging lobe was large – in proportion to the whole ear. The lobe was pierced three times. Twice with ruby studs and once with a delicate cross of gold. She sucked in her lower lip. Her eyes were blinking at the television. She hadn't watched the earlier sex bits – it was her brother after all.

"How did you get the video?" Shane asked.

"I've been opening Andrew's mail since I moved in," she said, staring at the stretch of carpet between her feet and the television. Nuala was blushing. Shane could even see it in the shadows.

"You've been what? Why?"

"I don't know . . . it's just my thing. He has a lot of work colleagues and bum-chums and whale enthusiasts – very sad lot. But I suppose if you're good with sad people then you'll never lack a friend. Simple really. I liked knowing his little secrets . . . the porno tapes he ordered from the continent and hid in his room. Well, he didn't hide them – he stored them in a drawer. I know everything about Andrew. I liked it that way. Even after I intercepted this tape."

Shane swept aside the curtains. Daylight streamed in and obscured the fuzzy interference on the TV screen. He absent-mindedly picked up the tarantula's glass case.

Nuala looked up. Her eyes were watered. She smiled and snuffled her nose. "He'd go to work long before me and then the post would come. I just steamed the interesting ones. It was easy – but you've gotta be careful in case you dampen the envelope too much and then it stains. But in some ways I'm a fucking perfectionist."

Shane sat down again. "Why didn't you – why didn't you confront him or tell the cops – all the things you should've done?"

"He's my brother, stupid. One day . . . Andrew told me that he had a deep secret to tell me. But of course I knew it wasn't a deep secret. It was a dirty secret. So I – I met you instead, outside in the car. It was then that I decided something had to be done. But nothing was certain. Nothing was certain until we were in the park today and then I knew that murder could be so fucking easy. But just in case I didn't kill him I had another note with me. To tell him everything. See, I suppose I knew all along that I wasn't going to *do it*."

"Another note? What the fuck are you talking about?"

"Oh nothing. The notes don't matter any more."

Shane looked out the window. He expected blue lights and *waa-waa* sirens. Instead there were just kids kicking a football. "It isn't easy to kill someone," he whispered.

"Yes, it is," Nuala stated. Then she asked, "So . . . what about you?"

Shane stretched his legs. They acted as arbitrator to his personal space. "I don't like to think about it."

Nuala smiled and exhaled her smoke with an enchantress's stare. Her cigarette dangled from her mouth and she spoke around it. "*Think about it*. Here . . . I'll do it for you. Your girlfriend dies – well, you kill her. You *did* kill her – from what you told me. You pushed her into wearing tampons and that was that."

Shane could feel his redness. He could never tell

whether Nuala was a queen of inclemency or perfect honesty. Shane stared towards Nuala but not at her. His vision was a blur. He was lost in her asseverations. There was an itch on his face. Just below his left eye. He raised a finger to scratch and it just smeared a tear. The shock of moisture shot Nuala into focus. "Yeah, you're right," he muttered. He listened to his voice and hated its frailty. He coughed to clear his voice with a boom of authority. "And what about you? This isn't all about Andy. You can't do those kind of things out of the blue, even if you're a woman and . . . protecting kids or whatever. Why let it build up and up until you drive a wooden log into the back of your brother's head?" Shane inhaled. That felt good. It was like hitting her. Hitting her hard.

"Mind your own business." Nuala checked her watch. Her eyes squinted as her brain did some type of calculation.

"What's on your mind?" Shane asked.

"What's on my mind? Neurones and neurones and millions more neurones and how we're all just eight-percent genetically different from fish. And whenever I die, the world will keep spinning. It's never over. The physics just won't stop." Nuala sighed. She seemed to ponder something. "OK – my secret is that I don't know if my Dad . . . the worst thing about me, the thing I hate most about me – actually the *only* thing I hate about me, is that there's a distinct possibility that I'm just another element of the molestation-generation."

"Jesus," Shane said.

"I asked my brother what used to happen at night when he was young and Andrew said that Dad used to come in and tuck him into bed. Every night. I – I hassled Andrew in a subtle way. I didn't let him get off the topic or weave around it. If anything had happened to him, he would have had to know what I was getting at. But no reaction. Nothing but eventual irritation. Dad just went to his room every night and tucked him in."

"So that's OK then?"

"He came to my room too. And tucked me in."

"Is that all?"

"No."

Shane leaned forward and growled, "That fucking prick."

"Don't call Dad names. I don't know what went on."

"Blackouts? Selective memories?" Shane scratched his head and searched for another term. "Or whatever?"

"No. I remember it all. He'd come in and peel back the bedclothes. Just to about my waist. And he'd touch my back. Always through my pyjamas. He'd just rub, softly, *his* type of softly, which means clumsily. He'd do this for a few minutes and then leave. The last night – before he died – he put his hand up my pyjama top and rubbed my bare back. That's all. For the first time I spoke to him while he did it. Didn't say much. Later he was dead . . . like I told you."

"Nice way to go, though. Sitting on a chair, reading the paper late at night and then it's over. Painless, no fear."

Nuala sighed and said, "Does touching your daughter's back *every* night constitute molestation? Was he just being tender in his clumsy big-handed way? What was he thinking? Was he thinking, 'Sweet dreams, Noodles'? Was he thinking, 'This is as far as I can go'? What if his . . . his thrill was just backs. Like my back. Human backs. Then . . . what's the difference between him and a father who likes his daughter's bottom? And maybe he was just saying goodnight every night. A big clumsy-handed goodnight."

"I'm sure he was," Shane said and swallowed. He hated not knowing what to say.

"Get up," Nuala said. She was already on her feet. She shook her head vigorously, her lips making a noise as if drying out her face. "I hate afternoon slumps. Look, I've things to do. I'm moving. Back to Mam's."

"You're moving . . . well yeah, that makes sense. Want a hand?"

"Nah, you've already moved most of my stuff for me. Remember those black sacks. Anyway, look . . . how can I say this? Give me a ring some time, yeah?" Nuala made the sign of the mobile before her mouth with her thumb and little finger.

Shane smiled. He loved it when she did that. He raised his fist to return the gesture and smacked himself in the mouth with the glass case it still clutched. "Oh Jesus," he mumbled and groaned. The glass had splintered and cut his lip. The pain pounded into his brain.

Nuala looked on with horror. "Lenny!" She grabbed the smashed case from his hand and petted a hairy leg. It broke off. "He's dead. Fuck." Nuala smiled sadly and dropped the case to the floor. "I wonder when he passed away," she mumbled.

"Shit, sorry," Shane said with a slight lisp. He didn't like the taste of his own blood.

"Look, Shane." She placed her strong hands on his cheeks and stared her unremarkable blue eyes into his. "We're through. *Finito*. I don't love you. I do like you. But now that we know everything about each other, we're just . . . we're already beginning to bore each other. Find someone else. What other reasons are there? Oh yeah – do it because you *can* do it. There you go, Shane – that was an optimistic statement from a *very* frequent pessimist."

Shane felt faint. The blood from his split lip pooled beneath his tongue. Nuala couldn't be finishing it, he thought. "You can't be finishing it," he said and swallowed.

"Your teeth are red," Nuala said and shook her head. "But yeah, that's it. I don't want to see you ever again. I'll think of you though. Promise."

Shane looked at his right elbow. Nuala was clutching it. He was moving forward, out of the living-room and into the hall. The front door opened and he stepped through the porch and outside to a summer's evening. Nuala was no longer holding his elbow. He turned around.

Nuala was standing in the hall. She smiled at Shane and began to clean an ear with her little finger. Then she shut the door.

Shane listened to his own breathing. It went on and on and on. He told himself to catch his thoughts. But his mind wasn't speeding. It wasn't even moving.

Chapter Twelve

THREE DAYS LATER

Everything about the hospital repelled Andrew. Seeping city smog darkened the main dreary roman-arced entrance and its adjacent hall's olive-coloured vaulted ceiling. It made the hospital look like a draconian building that one would only ever enter once. But he made a big deal of eating the food without fuss even though it tasted like the baked plastic of airline food.

Andrew was sitting up in the narrow iron hospital bed in a square white room. He jealously fingered the remote control. The tick-tock boredom was intolerable. There was nothing else to do besides flick around until he could find someone else to live his life for him. He continued flicking channels despite Eddie's occasional throaty groan from the bed beside him. Most of Eddie's head was in a cast, and wire scaffolding was built around a bruised opening that used to be his mouth. His head was slightly lowered against the world's constant presence. The hospital staff seemed to think that it was a good idea to have the victims of gay bashing incarcerated in the same room.

"Yoo-hoo!" Liam called from the open door.

Immediately Andrew tossed the control over to Eddie's bed. Because Eddie couldn't move his head he groped blindly for it before flicking from the National Geographic Channel to MTV with a hoarse sigh of relief.

"Ed," Liam said with a nod as he walked by. He pulled up a chair beside Andrew's bed and whispered, "Good old Eddie, such a bright future behind him."

"Hi," Andrew said and greedily began rooting through the plastic bag Liam had brought in. GQ, *Playgirl*, a bag of Liquorice All Sorts and a bottle of Calvin Klein after-shave. Andrew popped the lid and inhaled. When he was a young boy he'd always breathed deeply when in his mother's presence. He could never get enough of her perfume.

"That should get you by until tomorrow," Liam said and cracked his fingers. "Feeling better, man?"

"What do you think?"

"Just trying to be nice," Liam said and impatiently extracted a cigarette before remembering where he was and putting it away again. "Sometimes I think you act all superior just so no one will know that you're actually a moron."

Andrew was stunned. He turned his head so Liam could see the shaved patch and the rows of stitches.

"Sorry, Andy," Liam said and fidgeted with the cigarette box.

"It's all right," Andrew said. "I'm the one who owes you." Andrew had tried to walk out of the park but it soon became apparent that he couldn't even stand up. So he rang Liam on his mobile and Liam had come straight away to the rescue. Andrew tried hard to appear grateful.

"Andy, I really need a cigarette." Liam was already on his feet and on his way to the door. "I'll be back up in five minutes."

"I'll be waiting," Andrew muttered. He reached under his pillow and withdrew a yellow A4 page and reread its contents for the hundredth time.

Brother, as you've now probably guessed, I didn't kill you. I could have though. I know about Berlin. I have your little home/car made movie. Now we're quits. Well you're quits. I've moved out. Back to Mam's. I never want to talk to you again. I mean it. You can e-mail me though. Keep it brief. Scared you with those letters – ha, ha, ha. I should be an actress. But that was part of the payback. For the kid in Berlin. Oh yeah – and for not pretending to be straight for Mam and Dad's sake. For your own sake. To get yourself back into the house. You should have been there that night. Instead you were off with boys. You left everything to me. Everything.

Liam was back. "Chin up, Eddie," he chirped before sitting down beside Andrew. "So you're out of here in three days. Still thinking of America? Thought it might be the concussion talking. But if you are . . . I might be persuaded –"

"I don't know, Liam. Maybe I'll set up a kingdom on one of those icebergs the size of a country that keep breaking away from the Ross Ice Shelf."

Liam looked at Andrew with a stare that reached only a foot into the world.

Andrew gently rested his head back into his pillow and

sighed. He knew he wasn't going to go anywhere but home to Hill View Estate. All I want is internal quiet, he thought, and all I get is internal noise. I can never be where I want to be. Elsewhere is wherever I am.

Nuala snuggled deeper into the daffodil yellow eiderdown of her old bed. The bright sunlight made the blackness behind her eyelids turn red. She stretched and yawned with utter relaxation. The bedroom door opened. Nuala listened to her mother cross the room and place the rattling tray onto the flat of her bedside locker.

"Hi, Mam," Nuala said and shuffled her body into a half-upright position against the headboard.

"Oh, you're awake, pet. I didn't want to disturb you."

"Only dull people sleep easy, Mam."

"Look at the state of your room. You're only back a few days and a bomb could have hit it. Bits of that computer thingamajig everywhere. And those knickers! Put them out of sight. They're criminal."

Nuala rubbed her eyes and sniffed her coffee. Perfect. As good as Andrew's. "Don't worry, Mam, I sin in order to qualify for repentance."

"I suppose that's one of the things that little stick of a fella sees in you . . . what's his name? Shawn?"

"Oh, that's over. Just two ships passing, blah, blah, blah."

For a second Nuala's mother portrayed a vague relief as if she'd just seen someone slip on ice. Then she said, "Well, you're running out of time. No one's going to want to have babies with an old spinster living with her mother."

Nuala grunted and said, "Exactly what the world needs – another fucking mouth to feed."

"Nuala!"

"Sorry, Mam. God, I'm running late. How am I going to get to Nuala's Moonage Daydream for nine?"

Her mother retreated to the bedroom door. "Try clicking your heels three times, pet."

"Ha, ha," Nuala said and picked up a thick slice of toast dripping in butter and raised it to her mouth. With a wide smirk her teeth sank into it. Amazing, she thought. Even better than Andrew's.

THE END